Maxton eyed her and asked, "Isn't there something I didn't get to see?"

Teagan smiled. "If you mean my bedroom, you gotta earn it, playboy."

He laughed. "You're going to make me work for this. I just know it."

Her answer was a sultry smile. "We'll just have to see what happens."

"So, what are we doing here?"

"A fling? A dalliance? I don't think it matters what we call it, so long as we both understand what it is...and what it isn't."

Their gazes met and held, and the sparkle of mischief in her eyes threatened to do him in. "Enlighten me, Teagan. What will we be doing, exactly?"

"We hang out...have a little fun. No strings, no commitments. And above all, we don't let this thing interfere with our work or our lives." She pressed her open palm against his chest. "That is, if you think you can handle it."

* * *

After Hours Temptation by Kianna Alexander
is part of the 404 Sound series.

Dear Reader,

I'm so glad to have you along for the ride on this installment of my 404 Sound series. It's time for Teagan, the baby of the storied Woodson family, to meet her match. But will edgy musician Maxton McCoy prove too much for her? Family secrets are being revealed, drama is all around, and Max and Teagan will have to navigate it all while dealing with their own emotional turmoil. I hope you enjoy this story as much as I enjoyed torturing my characters, LOL.

All the best,

Kianna

KIANNA ALEXANDER

AFTER HOURS TEMPTATION

HARLEQUIN®
DESIRE™

Recycling programs
for this product may
not exist in your area.

ISBN-13: 978-1-335-73572-0

After Hours Temptation

Harlequin Enterprises ULC
22 Adelaide St. West, 41st Floor
Toronto, Ontario M5H 4E3, Canada
www.Harlequin.com

Printed in U.S.A.

Like any good Southern belle, **Kianna Alexander** wears many hats: doting mama, advice-dispensing sister, fun aunt and gabbing girlfriend. She's a voracious reader, an amateur seamstress, survival-horror gamer and occasional painter in oils. A native of the Tar Heel state, Kianna still lives there while maintaining her collection of well-loved vintage '80s Barbie dolls.

For more about Kianna and her books, visit her website at authorkiannaalexander.com, or sign up for Kianna's mailing list at authorkiannaalexander. com/sign-up/. You can also follow Kianna on social media: Facebook.com/kiannawrites, Twitter.com/ kiannawrites, Instagram.com/kiannaalexanderwrites and Pinterest.com/kiannawrites.

Books by Kianna Alexander

Harlequin Desire

404 Sound

After Hours Redemption
After Hours Attraction
After Hours Temptation

Visit her Author Profile page at Harlequin.com, or authorkiannaalexander.com, for more titles.

You can also find Kianna Alexander on Facebook, along with other Harlequin Desire authors, at Facebook.com/harlequindesireauthors!

For. The. Culture.

One

Leaning her ergonomic work chair as far back as it would go, Teagan Woodson turned the page in the manual she was reading. The LED lights overhead chased away the darkness in the sound booth, allowing her to read the words with ease despite the late hour. The manual, filled with all the details about the Harcroft Diamond Edition Digital Audio Workstation, wasn't exactly light reading, especially when she was this tired. Still, it had to be done. She was known for her adeptness with the sound equipment and she wasn't about to be caught lacking now.

She'd developed a certain fondness for the machine, and even gave it a nickname: Fancy.

Earlier in the week, a cloud-based update had been automatically installed on the system, adding several new features to the already impressive list of what the machine could do. That update, which was extensive enough to leave the system unavailable for an entire day, was her focus now. When the next artist came in to record, she'd be ready, because she knew this machine inside and out.

That artist would be the Bronx-based rapper Sherman "Lil Swagg" Washburn. Known for his recent hits with both new school artists like Paige the Princess, and legendary pioneers like Rakim, Swagg was making major moves in the hip-hop game. He'd come to 404 Sound seeking a full-service, boutique approach, and as the lead sound engineer, it was her job to provide him with the high-quality experience he expected.

She flipped a page, coming to the section on file backups and security. The manual had originally been a PDF file, loaded on to the system itself, but she'd had it printed and bound at the local office-supplies store. She found it easier to read on paper and figured it would be simpler to reference should the time ever come. She'd rather leaf through this 200-page, comb-bound book than scroll through as many pages on the workstation's screen looking for whatever small detail she needed.

She'd spent the better part of the last few months testing out the new equipment, ever since it had been installed. And while part of her felt nostalgic for Old Reliable, the original soundboard that had been in continuous use since the studio opened its doors in the early nineties, that nostalgia did little to dampen her excitement. Old Reliable was now carefully packaged in the storage room, pending physical refurbishment to her original glory. After that, the old board would be placed on display, as a cherished relic of 404's storied past.

The new workstation was top-of-the-line, and she knew she'd oversee the creation of countless hit songs and albums while operating it. She'd been slowly reading through the manual, trying out each feature as she came to it in the text.

She yawned, the breath escaping before she could free a hand to stifle it. She closed the manual and set it on the counter. Scooting her chair just outside the booth's door to the little side table in the hall, she took a sip of her now watered-down iced coffee before replacing it and scooting back inside again. She remembered her brother Gage calling her "extra" for her rule about not having any food or drinks within five feet of the counter, and chuckled. A red tape outline on the carpeted floor clearly marked out the "consumables exclusion zone," and she explained this policy to every single new person who entered the booth.

It might be extra, but I'm not having some slippery-fingered producer or artist manager spilling anything on my equipment. Because at the end of the day, this was Teagan's sound booth. She might be the baby of the storied Woodson family—and only because her impatient-ass twin brother had beat her into the world by three-and-a-half minutes—but she was still chief tech officer and master of this studio. In here, her word was law, and everyone knew it.

She stood, stretched. The workstation's on-screen clock showed the time: 8:32. Everyone else in the building was long gone by now, except maybe security and janitorial staff. She rubbed her eyes, trying to shake off the bleariness, but to no avail. *I've only got ten pages left in the manual. I'm just gonna push through.* She reopened the comb-bound book, flipping the pages back to where she'd left off.

A few lines in, she heard the telltale click-clack generated only by a pair of heels on the tile floor in the hallway.

She stopped reading, turning her chair around to see her big sister, Nia, coming into the room, pausing in the door frame. Dressed in her typical attire of black cigarette pants and a matching blazer with a soft pink blouse, she looked professional and stylish.

Teagan swept her eyes over her sister, then glanced down at her own gray tunic, black leggings and ballet flats, once again realizing that the two daughters of the Woodson family resided on opposite ends of the fashion spectrum. Nia was all about polish and panache, while she craved comfort and quirk above all else; Nia stuck to 1-carat studs, while Teagan preferred long, flashy dangling earrings that caught the light just right.

Nia eyed her questioningly as she leaned against the door frame. "What are you doing here so late?"

"I could ask you the same thing," Teagan quipped.

"Touché, I guess." Nia chuckled. "But you know a CEO's work is never finished."

"You're the literal boss, sis. You could go home anytime you want. You're just too much of a control freak to delegate anything."

Nia rolled her eyes. "Whatever. Get your stuff. I'm going home, and you should, too."

She glanced at the manual lying open on her lap. Knowing her sister wouldn't take no for an answer, she closed it and set it on the counter. She took a few moments to shut down the equipment, then gathered her purse and keys. Turning the lights off inside the recording suite, she locked the door behind her as she left.

Moments later, she was following Nia as her fast-walking elder sister strode down the corridor. Nia's giant, long-legged steps had always been a thorn in Teagan's side; even fully grown, she was still two inches shorter than her Amazonian sister. She'd always been like that; Teagan's first memories of her sister were of her striding across the house and the yard, and of her barking orders at all the other siblings. Teagan knew her sister loved them all, but she also knew her sister was way too serious.

"Slow down, Nia. You walking or skating?"

Nia laughed but didn't slow down as she breezed through the studio's front door.

Outside in the parking lot, they stood by Nia's car. "Any plans tonight?"

Teagan chuckled. "You ask that as if I have a social life."

Her lips pursed momentarily before she spoke again. "Look, Teagan. I'm the oldest and the highest-ranking among all the siblings. Every day, I feel the weight of the responsibility for the success of this company bearing down on my shoulders, and that's why I work as hard as I do." She paused. "You, on the other hand, are young and carefree. You should be dating. Or at least attempting to."

She sighed. "You sound just like Mom. Did she put you up to this?"

Nia shook her head. "No, of course not. I haven't even talked to her today."

She didn't know if she believed that. "Interesting, because Mom said basically the same thing to me a couple of weeks ago."

"That's probably because she sees it, too. I know it isn't easy, but try not to shut yourself off from the rest of the world too much."

"Gee, you're laying it on thick, aren't you? You make it seem like what I do isn't important. Without a sound engineer and tech officer, this place wouldn't last a week."

"I know, sis. I'm not trying to discount your importance around here. We definitely need you. Nobody understands the sound equipment as well as you." Nia opened the driver's-side door of her black luxury sedan. "But you can work hard here and still have a personal life."

"And you?" Teagan raised a brow as she waited for her sister's response.

Nia shrugged. "One day. It's not a priority for me right now... Maybe after the anniversary celebration."

"What a cop-out." Teagan shook her head. "I think I'll wait, too, then."

"Look around, sis. Blaine and Gage are already happily married, and nobody saw that coming." She winked as she got into her car and shut the door. She started the engine and called through the open window, "You never know when love will come around."

"Neither do you," Teagan shot back as her sister backed out of her parking space.

Heading down a few spaces, she got into her own car, a white coupe, and fired up the engine, pulling out onto the road behind her sister. At the next light, they parted ways as Nia took a left, headed for her house in the Westview neighborhood Teagan took a right, toward Shimmering Lakes, the quiet, well-established housing area she lived in.

Driving through the brightly lit streets of Atlanta, she thought about her sister's words. It was so funny that everyone thought she could just...go out. As if exploring the city and the world, beyond the safety of the places and people she knew, came easy to her. She might seem like she could conquer anything, but no one had any idea how much work it took to appear that way.

Shaking her head, she pulled into her driveway,

pushing her mother and sister's well-meaning but annoying admonishments out of her mind.

Jogging through the front door of his second-story studio apartment, Maxton McCoy locked it behind him. Hanging the keys on the hook mounted nearby, he swiped his hand over his head, knocking down the hood of his jacket as he ran his hand over his sweat-dampened hair. The endorphin high from his four-mile run around the neighborhood still lingered, making him smile as he shuffled his feet, shifting weight from one foot to the other.

The thumping bass and fast-paced lyrics of legendary Cali rapper E-40 filled his ears as the workout playlist saved to his phone continued to resonate. The Vallejo-born lyricist, known for tongue-twisting rhymes, was often credited with helping solidify the Bay area's importance in hip-hop culture. E-40's unique style, along with his contributions, placed him at the top of Maxton's list of favorite artists.

Walking over to the area just beyond his sofa, he sat down on the throw rug. He could feel the sweat running down his body beneath his clothing and was beyond ready for a shower, but he knew if he didn't do his push-ups and sit-ups now, they wouldn't get done.

He got into position, and with the music still blasting in his ears, did his customary one hundred push-ups. That done, he flipped over and lay on his back, beginning his one hundred sit-ups.

Suddenly, E-40's rapping ceased, and the sound of his phone's ringer filled his ears, accompanied by strong vibrations in the hip pocket of his sweatpants. Lying on his back, he tapped the button on the side of his headphones to answer the call. "Hello?"

"Hey, man. What's up?"

He smiled, recognizing his friend's voice right away. "Hey, Sharrod. Nothing going on here but them post-run sit-ups. What's going on with you, my dude?"

Sharrod chuckled. "Still going out for those three-mile runs, even though nobody chasing your ass?"

"Nah, today I ran four miles, smart-ass. That bass is heavier than most people think it is. Gotta keep my upper-body strength intact."

"I guess you don't wanna be caught lacking on-stage, huh?"

"Hell, nah, dude." He laughed. "Where are you?"

"I'm still in Atlanta. I'm staying at Aunt Judy's place over in Greenbriar."

"Oh, yeah, yeah. I'm still here, too. I took a three-month lease on a studio over here near Virginia Highlands."

Sharrod paused. "Really? You mean you decided to stick around instead of taking off?" His tone of voice conveyed his surprise.

"Yeah, I stayed." Maxton would be the first to admit that he'd lived a life on the go, constantly in motion, from one city to the next. All that had changed eight months ago, when one astronomical loss had rocked his entire world.

"Didn't see that coming. You usually up and disappear as soon as we finish a tour, either to set up for the next one or to visit some faraway place."

Maxton held back a sigh. "Nah, man. I just…don't feel like chasing anything right now, you know?"

"You getting old on me, man." He paused as if realizing. "Oh, shit. Man, I'm sorry. I shouldn't have…"

"It's okay, dude. No worries." Though he and Sharrod had been friends since their college days, he didn't expect him to be able to read his mind. He kept the pain of that day well hidden, and though Sharrod was aware of it, they rarely spoke of the incident.

Sharrod's nervous chuckle broke the silence. "How did you find a place that'd let you lease for only three months?"

"Paying it all up-front in cash probably worked in my favor," Maxton quipped, sitting up and stretching his arms over his head, relieved by his friend's desire to change the direction of their conversation to a lighter topic. "I figured, since we just finished up with Naiya B's first major tour, that I'd just hang here for a bit and see what gig comes my way."

"Yeah, I was thinking the same thing. Aunt Judy's rarely ever home. Right now she's up in Jersey with her sorority sisters. So I knew she wouldn't mind me crashing here until somebody needs a drummer."

"Plenty of artists down here, so it's bound to be

some work for us soon." Maxton climbed to his feet and crossed the apartment to the kitchen area. There, he pulled down his single-serve mixer and the container of protein powder from his upper cabinets, then grabbed the almond milk from his stainless steel refrigerator, setting everything on the black granite countertop.

"I thought you'd have to haul ass back down here, but this is perfect," Sharrod said. "We've already got a potential gig."

Adding the milk and powder to the mixer, Maxton felt his brow scrunch in confusion. "It's Tuesday, bruh, and our last gig just ended Saturday night. What do you mean we already have something lined up?"

"I was on the Gram yesterday, and I saw a post by Lil Swagg."

Maxton put the lid on the mixer and pressed the button, searching his memory bank for that name as the motor whirred quietly. "Is he the kid that did the song with Cambria and Paige the Princess? The one about sex in a limo?"

"'Freeway Threeway.' Yeah, that's him. Anyway, he's holding open auditions for musicians to be on his upcoming album, and he posted a link to a sign-up form."

Turning off the mixer, he disconnected the cup from the base and took a sip. The thick concoction didn't taste nearly as chocolaty as the commercial promised, but protein shakes rarely did. "Let me guess. You signed us both up, right?"

"Yep. And it's a good thing, because the sign-ups were full within ten minutes of him posting the link." Sharrod cleared his throat. "Bet you're glad I'm always lurking on social media right about now, huh?"

He shook his head, thinking back on the times he'd chastised his friend for being too plugged into the newsfeeds and timelines of various social sites, obsessively following the lives of the wealthy and well-connected. "I mean, a broken clock is right twice a day, so..."

"Whatever. Stop hating. The auditions are Thursday morning at nine." He paused. "Swagg says he's looking for a unique sound that he can only get from a full band. If we want this gig, we gotta bring our A-game."

"Understood." Max took another long sip of the shake, hoping his muscles would appreciate it more than his taste buds did. "So, where are these auditions happening?"

Sharrod sounded as if he were reading when he answered, "At 404 Sound Recording Studios. Place up near Collier Heights."

Scratching his chin, Maxton nodded. "Oh, yeah. I've heard great things about that place. I know where it is."

"I've still got my rental car. Do you want me to pick you up?"

"That's fine." Finishing the shake, he set the cup

in the sink. "I would just take the MARTA, but if you come get me, I won't have to haul my bass on public transport."

"Cool. I'll be there around eight, then." Sharrod yawned. "Let me let you go. After all, you only got a day to get that bass sounding like something."

"Whatever, Sharrod. Do you even know where your sticks are right now?"

"Dude, you know they always in my hand." He tapped them together to prove his point.

"Well, the shower is calling my name so I'll holla at you later."

After disconnecting the call, Maxton took off his headphones, turned off the wireless link to his phone, and left them on the coffee table.

Walking across the apartment and past the dividing wall that separated his bedroom from the rest of the space, he went to the closet to grab clean clothes and a towel. On the way from the closet to the bathroom, he paused at his nightstand and looked at the framed photo displayed there.

He never bothered with decorating, because his work meant never staying in one place too long. If a lucrative touring gig came up, he needed to be ready to pack up and leave, sometimes with very little advance notice. He'd never even purchased a set of curtains or a houseplant. But this picture made wherever he was, no matter how short the duration of his stay, feel like home.

Inside the polished walnut frame was an old photo

of him and his family. It was taken when he was about seventeen. The four of them were dressed in white button-down shirts and blue jeans. His parents, archaeologist Dr. Stephen McCoy and anthropologist Dr. Wanda McCoy, smiled at him from the photo, as did his younger sister, Whitney. Lingering on her face made the sadness rise in his chest once again.

Right now, his parents were home in Calabasas, having recently returned from exploring the ruins at Pompeii. In the past, they'd have invited him along on the excursion; but they knew things were different now. Since they'd lost Whitney, the entire family dynamic had changed. His parents continued on with their travels in the name of science, and he threw himself into his work.

There'd been a time when he chased adventures, just like his parents had raised him to do. Now he played it safe, colored inside the lines. One event had changed him, made him flee from the risks he once took so freely.

Two

Teagan walked into the recording suite around eight Thursday morning after depositing her iced coffee from the Bodacious Bean on the table just outside the door. Flipping on the lights, she hung her bag on the little metal hanger affixed to the bottom of the counter and sat down on her chair. She'd dressed up a bit today, donning a flowing beige top, wide-legged jeans and brown leather platform heels. Since her hair rarely cooperated when it mattered, she'd wrestled it into a low bun at her nape and put on a pair of dangly gold earrings with a matching necklace.

In less than an hour, the room would be abuzz with activity. For right now, she just wanted to get set up, get her bearings and prepare for a full day at the soundboard.

She'd finished reading up on Fancy's latest updates and felt confident she could run the system properly. Turning on the workstation, she set it to run a system diagnostic. While she waited for it to display a report, she moved around the suite, making sure everything was in place. The custodial staff's handiwork was evident in the freshly vacuumed throw rug, the fluffed pillows on the sofa and the slight scent of lemon Pine Glo hanging in the air.

The sound of approaching footsteps drew her attention to the door, just in time to see Trevor, 404's sound engineer, entering. "Morning, Teagan."

"Morning, Trevor." She walked his way. "Everything good in Studio Two?"

He nodded, shrugging out of his denim jacket. "Yup. Just came from there, and the systems are up and running just fine. I don't anticipate any problem when Gage comes in later for his monthly check."

"Awesome. You know what a stickler my brother is." She shook her head, thinking how little marriage had mellowed him when it came to organizational stuff. "Anyway, can you head on into the booth and set up for these auditions? I'm expecting Swagg, his manager and the musicians to start showing up pretty soon."

"No problem." After hanging his jacket up on one of the three silver hooks just inside the door, he walked past her and opened the interior door to the sound booth.

Teagan sat down at the workstation, watching

through the glass as Trevor checked the connections on the various speakers, amplifiers and microphones inside the booth, then adjusted the position of the electrical cords so they wouldn't be in the middle of the floor. He stopped near the microphone, signaling her with his hand.

She engaged the booth's audio system to talk to him. "Give me a sec. I'm still waiting on diagnostics."

He nodded. "I'm gonna do a soundproofing check real quick." He moved away from the mic, circling around the perimeter of the booth, examining the foam barrier on the walls for any sign of damage.

The diagnostic report finally popped up on the screen, and Teagan made note of the pertinent details. The green icon at the end indicated everything was good with the software, so she closed the report and started up the main program. "Okay, Trevor. Give me a sound check, please."

He moved over to the mic and spoke into it. "Mic check, one, two, three."

She gave him the thumbs-up. "Test my headset for me, please. I'm gonna drop a beat." She waited for him to slip on the headset, then touched the screen to start up the last beat she'd played, a trap tune recently recorded by 2 Chainz and Lil Jon.

He nodded along to the beat and gave a thumbs-up.

"Thanks, Trevor. You can come on out now."

He exited the booth. "Looks like you're all good

for recording today. I'll head up to reception and help direct the musicians your way."

"Thanks," she called as he grabbed his jacket and made his way out.

She ducked out long enough to take a long sip of iced coffee, then returned to the booth. As she shut off the music she'd played for the sound check, someone tapped on the door.

She turned and smiled. "Good Morning, Mr. Swagg."

Lil Swagg gave her a sparkling, gold-and-diamond-encrusted smile before replying. "What's up, shawty. Call me Swagg, no mister." A pair of sunglasses with blue lenses rested on top of his close-trimmed hair. He was dressed in an oversize gray T-shirt, designer jeans, a leather jacket and a pair of all-black running shoes. The heavy-looking gold chain around his neck had *Swagg* spelled out in black diamonds.

"Got it." She stood, noting that they were about evenly matched in height as she bumped fists with him. "I'm Teagan, chief tech officer and sound engineer. I'll be running your auditions today."

"Cool, cool." He looked over his shoulder, then looked back. "My manager is with me. He was behind me a minute ago." He ducked his head around the corner, calling down the corridor. "Aye, Rick! Hustle up, man!"

Another man appeared within a few moments. "Sorry 'bout that, Swagg. Had to take a call." He nodded in her direction. "Rick Royce." He was shorter and stockier than his client and dressed in khakis and a long-sleeved green polo with brown loafers.

"Nice to meet you, I'm Teagan. I'll be working with you today. Come on into the recording suite and make yourself comfortable."

As the two men moved past her in a haze of expensive-smelling cologne, Teagan returned to Fancy and opened up a new data set where she'd be saving the audition audio for Swagg and Rick's later review. Checking the time on-screen, she noted that it was about fifteen minutes until the official kickoff time for the auditions.

The echoing sounds in the hallway let her know that the group of musicians was approaching. Peeking out the door, she saw Trevor guiding a group of people into an orderly line in the corridor just beyond the recording suite. There were both men and women hauling various instrument cases and more than a few with drumsticks in hand.

She stood, knowing she'd need to inform the musicians of what to expect. Stopping in the doorway, she got a closer look at the man at the head of the line.

He looked tall, maybe three or four inches taller than she was. He had a medium complexion, and she could just see the ends of his short, curly hair peeking from beneath a black beret. A full beard covered his jawline, surrounding full lips that curved up into a half smile, and dark sunglasses obscured his eyes from view. He wore a red shirt with vertical black stripes beneath a silver-studded leather jacket, and a pair of inky-black jeans with studded, coal-colored combat boots. A large guitar case was slung over his shoulder, the strap cutting diagonally across his chest.

As if noticing her attention, he removed the glasses and tucked them into an inner jacket pocket. His soulful hazel eyes met hers.

Is it my imagination, or is he staring at me, too?

She swallowed, trying to shake off the ribbon of heat that snaked down her spine. "Hi, everyone. We'll be calling you into the recording suite in groups, by instrument. Swagg has asked for you in this order, so please line up this way. Bassists, guitarists, keyboardists, drummers."

She waited while the group readjusted themselves; Mr. Dark Glasses held on to his spot in the front. *So he's a bass player.* For some reason, it thrilled her to learn that little tidbit about him.

"I want to make you aware that there is no food, drinks or smoking allowed in the recording suite. I'll also ask that you keep quiet while the sessions are in progress. These rules are in place to protect both the integrity of my equipment and of the creative process." She cleared her throat. "I'll begin calling you in shortly. For now, just hang tight." She turned and retreated back into the recording suite, away from the bassist's arresting gaze.

From his seat on the couch, Swagg announced, "I'm ready for the bass players, shawty."

Teagan nodded. "First bass player in line, come on in."

The man in the beret entered, pausing in the doorway. He was close enough now for her to smell the rich, woodsy scent rolling off of him.

"What's your name?" She looked at the printed list on the counter.

"Maxton McCoy."

She crossed his name off. "Go ahead into the booth and set up your bass."

He nodded to her and did as she asked.

She watched through the glass as he opened his case and plugged it into the amp. Taking a seat on one of the three stools in the booth, he donned the headphones and gave a thumbs-up.

She enabled the recording function, then started the track he was to play along with. While his fingers worked over the strings, she found she couldn't take her eyes off his face. His eyes were closed as if the music had snatched him out of this dimension and into another, where only creative flow existed.

Despite the pleased reactions from Swagg and Rick, and the overall purpose of the moment, one thought overrode all.

Damn, he's fine.

In the cool, dim interior of the booth, Maxton listened to the sound coming over his headphones for a few beats. It was a stripped-down, freestyle performance of one of Swagg's songs, one he hadn't heard and assumed was unreleased. The arrangement included only the rapper's voice and a basic treble melody.

The song itself had a brooding tone, and he knew it would require some minor chords to really bring out its meaning. He wriggled and stretched his fingers but didn't pluck the strings just yet, giving himself a bit more time to fully absorb the vibe.

His ears were analyzing the music, but his eyes were on the sound engineer.

In his ten-plus years of touring and recording, he'd only come across a handful of female engineers, but that wasn't what held his attention about her. She was beautiful in a way that almost hurt his eyes. She didn't seem to be wearing any makeup, and she had clear skin, high cheekbones and sparkling brown eyes. Her curly hair was tucked into a low bun, and based on the level of focus she demonstrated at the controls, he could see why. She seemed like the type to concentrate more on her work than her appearance, not that she needed to make much effort in that department. She was already radiant.

Once he wrestled his focus back and picked up on the tone and cadence of the rap, he started working his fingers over the four strings of Joan, his Fender American Professional II Precision Bass. He'd been playing this particular instrument for the last four years, having upgraded from the previous model. He loved everything about it, from the satiny-smooth feel of the rosewood fingerboard to the vintage-style, steel-and-brass bridge to the subtle, just-right curve of the neck board. Right down to the vibrant, three-color sunburst finish, it fit his exacting tastes and playing style like no other left-handed bass on the market.

He settled into the rhythm, nodding his head along with Swagg's voice as he kept time. The rap, a serious one about the pain of losing a friend to violence in the streets, hit home for him in a way he hadn't expected. Rather than try to tamp down his rising emotions, though, he let them have their moment, using them to infuse his interpretation with something real, something that transcended sound and became feeling.

He closed his eyes as his fingers flowed over the strings in time with the song, keeping a steady bass line while adding improvisation to moments he felt could use it. The vibration from his bass traveled through his fingertips and his hands, up to his arms and down into his chest, carrying him away to another dimension. He always felt like this when he played, and he'd come to truly enjoy this glorious escape into his art.

Anticipating the approaching end of the track, he finished with a flourish and let his bass drop softly at his side. Opening his eyes, he set his gaze once again on the gorgeous woman working the sound equipment.

She gave him a soft smile and a thumbs-up.

He took off the headphones, hung them back on

their hook and packed up his bass. Then he exited the booth and approached Swagg, who was gesturing to him.

"That was amazing. You definitely got talent, homie." Swagg stuck out his hand.

"Thanks." Maxton shook his hand. "I appreciate that."

"What's your background? Like, who've you played for?"

"Mostly R & B and soul artists. Johnny Gill, Jaheim, Usher, Charlie Wilson, Lloyd."

Swagg nodded. "Yeah, I can definitely hear that in the way you play. I like your style." He gave Max a pat on the arm. "We'll be in touch with you, playa."

"Thanks again." Maxton started for the door, stepping aside to let the next bass player in before leaving the recording suite.

In the corridor, he sat down on the floor and propped his bass against the wall. The spot he'd chosen gave him a clear view of the beautiful woman sitting at the board.

Sharrod, still in line, said, "Man, why don't you go sit in the reception area or wait in the car?"

He shook his head. "Nah, man. I think I'm good here." He was content to watch the engineer work until she had a little free time between auditions to talk. She might shoot him down, but before he left the building, he had to at least know her name.

He watched the other bassists, then the guitarists enter in turn, all while wondering what made her tick. How had she gotten interested in sound engineering? How long had she been working for the board? How old was she? Did she have a man?

Those last two weren't really any of his business, and he definitely wouldn't lead with them, but for the moment, his curiosity was getting the better of him.

When Sharrod exited after completing his audition, Maxton was standing. "How'd it go?"

Sharrod shrugged. "Pretty good, from what I can tell. Swagg complemented my stick work, so…"

"He had some compliments for me too, so maybe we'll both get the gig." Maxton slapped his friend on the shoulder. "Go on out to the car. I gotta take care of something real quick."

Sharrod frowned. "What are you doing, dude?"

"Don't worry 'bout it." He passed him his instrument case. "Take this with you, bruh. Just put it in the back seat."

"I'm not your butler, you know," he groused. But he took the case anyway and, with a shake of his head, walked away.

Maxton folded his arms across his chest, leaned against the wall and waited for the recording suite to empty out. Swagg and his manager were the last to leave. Swagg extended his fist as he passed. "Thanks for auditioning, homie."

He bumped fists with the young lyricist. "Thanks for the opportunity." Once they were gone, he returned his attention to the recording suite. The engineer was still seated at the monitor, and he could see her typing and clicking away.

Entering the room slowly, he asked, "Do you have to keep working much longer?"

"Not much longer." She glanced up, then went right back to what she was working on. "Just running a few file backups."

He could hear heavy footsteps approaching but chose to ignore the sound. "So, what's your name?"

She opened her mouth, then closed it. Her gaze shifted as if she were looking behind him.

He turned and saw a man standing about six inches behind him. He was tall, of medium complexion and was dressed in a white button-down and khakis. His arms were folded tightly over his broad chest, and his strangely familiar face was folded into a serious expression.

Not knowing what else to say, Maxton said, "Hi."

The man looked right past him to the sound engineer. "Teagan, is he bothering you?"

She chuckled. "Not really."

"Are you sure? Because my twin sense was tingling, and I picked up the distinct feeling of annoyance." He glared at Max.

"It's fine, Miles, so take a chill pill." She shook her head. "This is Maxton, one of the bassists that Lil Swagg auditioned today."

Miles stuck out his hand. "Hello, Maxton. I apologize for my manners. I'm just protecting my twin sister. I'm sure you understand."

"Of course I do," Max said, shaking hands with him. After all, he'd once been that way with Whitney. Tamping down the sadness that often accompanied thoughts of her, he turned his mind back to the matter at hand. *So they're twins?* "You're identical, right?"

"Yep. Right down to the birthmark." Teagan turned her head slightly to the left, revealing a dark, jagged mark on her throat. Maxton turned to see Miles tug down his collar to reveal the same mark.

"Kinda looks like a lightning bolt." Maxton scratched his chin.

"Yes. And if you harm my sister, I'll bring the thunder." Miles smiled, but it didn't quite reach his eyes.

"Noted." Maxton wasn't sure how he felt about this whole situation, but at least he'd gotten an answer to his question, in a roundabout way.

"So, you're alright?" Miles asked his sister.

"Yes, so go on back to…whatever it is you usually do upstairs." She waved him off with her hand.

He shrugged. "Okay, as long as you're good, I'm good." Miles turned and walked down the corridor toward the elevators.

Once Miles was gone, Teagan said, "Sorry about that. You share a womb with someone, and they get a little overprotective, I guess."

Maxton chuckled. "No big deal. At least now I know your name."

She gave him a crooked half smile. "And why

were you so interested in knowing my name, by the way?"

He rubbed his hands together. "I just thought it would be good to establish some rapport with you. Since we're going to be working together soon."

She tilted her head to one side, her brow furrowed. "Swagg auditioned five bassists today. What makes you so sure you'll be chosen?"

"I just know. It's hard to explain." He tugged his lapels, pulling his jacket closer around his body. "I don't want to hold you up from your work, so I'll see you later, Ms. Teagan."

She rolled her eyes. "No miss, please. Just Teagan."

"See, look at that. We've established a dynamic already." With a wink, he turned and walked away.

Outside, he opened the passenger-side door of Sharrod's rented sedan and climbed inside.

Seated in the driver's seat, Sharrod asked, "Did you take care of whatever you stuck around for?"

He nodded. "Yeah, bro. I think I did."

"You care to elaborate on that?"

"Nah." Maxton turned toward the window and smiled.

Three

Teagan sank into the soft, buttery leather of the pedicure chair and immediately reached for the remote. Turning on the chair's massage function, she adjusted the speed and pattern to her liking, then leaned back to enjoy the sensations.

"Ah, I love these chairs," her sister, Nia, who was laid out in the chair next to her, commented. "That's why I always come here. They have the best pedicure chairs in town."

Teagan nodded her agreement. The interior of Nubian Nails and Spa was relatively quiet for a Friday, and she attributed that to the early afternoon hour. The summer sun played over the metallic flecks in the gold paint covering the walls and bounced off the glass fronting the framed African art prints. "I'm glad your half day lined up with my day off this month. If we had waited to come in after five, it would've been super packed in here."

Nia stifled a yawn. "Ever since Mom implemented these 'self-care half days' for me, I've mostly been rolling alone. I mean, she never asked the rest of you to take regular time off like this."

"We both know Mom didn't ask. She just told you." Teagan shook her head. Their mother Addison's strong yet loving presence meant she rarely had to force an issue with her children. "And she didn't make the rest of us do it because we actually take days off."

"Oh, hush." Nia held up her hands, showing off the French manicure she'd just had done on her natural nails. "I did my nails this time, too, so lay off me. I'm maxing and relaxing, just as Mom demands."

Teagan looked at her own full set of medium-length, almond-shaped gel nails in a pinkish-nude color. "I really like how mine turned out. And I'm glad I took the tech's advice and added a little bling to my ring fingers."

"Nah, you know me. If my nails are too long or have too much embellishment, it just slows me down at work."

Staring at her older sister, Teagan wondered if she ever stopped thinking about work. "Were you just, like, born this serious, or did you acquire it before I was born?"

She shrugged. "Probably the first one. There's

five of us. At least one of us has to be practical and responsible."

"Don't worry, I think you and Gage have that covered."

The nail technicians began filling the tubs of the pedicure chairs with steaming water, essential oils and flower petals. Teagan inhaled deeply as the scents of lavender, citrus and sage floated past her nostrils. At her tech's prompting, she placed her feet in the water and sighed as the heat enveloped them. The combination of the vibration of the chair and the hot water threatened to send her straight to dreamland, but her sister's voice postponed the trip.

"It's been such a crazy week. I've spent these last several days chasing down data for the second quarter reports that are due by next Tuesday."

"I know, Nia. I submitted the data from the technology department already."

"Yeah, you did, and I appreciate you being on time. But not all the departments were so fastidious." She ran a hand over her short-cropped hair. "It was pretty touch-and-go for a moment, but I did get the last departmental report this morning. I think we're in line now to have everything ready for the Q2 meeting on Wednesday." She paused. "How are things going down in Studio One?"

"Nothing's happening right now. Lil Swagg booked the studio until the beginning of August, so on days like this when he's not recording, I don't have any reason to be there." The massage program ended, and she grabbed the remote to restart it. "Swagg decided to wait until Monday to replay the recordings and make a decision on which musicians to use in his backing band."

"Okay. But what's this I hear from Miles about one of the musicians lingering after the auditions were over?"

Teagan rolled her eyes. *Dimed out by my own twin. Ain't that a mess?* "The family grapevine strikes again, I see."

"The blessing and the curse of working in the family business." Nia laughed. "So, tell me about this guy. Miles didn't give me much."

She jerked a bit, trying not to laugh while the nail tech worked a pumice stone over the bottom of her foot. "There's not much to tell. We didn't even speak for five minutes before Miles showed up to bully him."

"Sounds like Miles. He's always been very protective of you." She shifted her position in the chair, leaning closer to her little sister. "What's his name?"

"His name is Maxton McCoy, and he's a bass player. He was the first one to audition in that group, and for some reason, he chose to stick around and talk to me after everyone else left."

Nia plucked her phone from the pocket of her denim shorts and began tapping the screen. "Go on. Tell me what he looks like."

"He's, uh, maybe three or four inches taller than me. Lighter complexion. He has this really great hair texture, this loose curl pattern that just sort of hangs down and frames his face." She paused, thinking back to her first look at him. "He has a great sense of style, kind of edgy. You know, the way Blaine used to dress back in the day before he toned it down. And he has the most gorgeous hazel eyes…" She stopped, realizing how much she'd already gone on about Maxton.

Nia stared. "Okay, sis. Seems like he's got some impressive qualities. How was his musicianship?"

"Really great, actually. It's been a while since I've had a bass player in the studio who was that young who had so much… I don't know…soul." She could still hear his playing in the back of her mind. "He's definitely got the chops."

Holding up her phone, Nia turned the screen to face her. "Is this him?"

Teagan balked when she saw Maxton's social media profile displayed on the screen. "Sheesh. Yes, that's him, ace detective Nia."

She nodded, drawing her phone back toward herself. "He's definitely handsome. I can see why you'd be attracted to him."

"Who said that?"

Nia laughed. "Sis, please. You wouldn't have described him the way you just did if you didn't find him attractive."

She looked away, unable to deny the truth in those words. "Fine. He's attractive, we can agree on that. But it doesn't matter."·

"Why not? Who says you and Mr. McCoy can't be a thing?"

She swallowed.

"What color did you want, honey?" the tech asked.

"Um, just match my nails, please." Teagan turned back to her sister. "I say we can't be a 'thing.' You and I have grown up in the music industry. We both know that musicians are flighty and unstable. They just don't know how to chill or settle down."

"Teagan, do you hear yourself? You sound like you've totally drunk the stereotype tea." Nia raised her seat back and eyed her.

"Whatever." She hit a button on the remote, matching her sister's posture.

"I'm not saying you have to marry him or anything. But why not have a little fun with a good-looking man who's interested in you?"

"Is that what you do, Nia? Have little, insignificant flings with guys?" She leaned forward, her eyebrows raised. "Because I'd love to hear about that."

Nia groaned. "You know I don't do that. I don't have time to date, let alone carry on a fling."

"Neither do I."

"Anyway, don't try to turn the question around on me. We're talking about you and your handsome, edgy bassist." Nia slipped her feet into the disposable sandals offered by her nail tech.

The two of them grabbed their purses and shoes and shuffled their way to the drying station, sitting down again. Teagan shivered a bit at the cool air being blown on her feet by the fans. "I haven't been on a date in ages. The quality of guys in Atlanta can be very variable, and that becomes even truer with just the men that hang around the studio for whatever reason."

"True enough." Nia sighed. "Look at us. Turning into two old spinsters while two of our brothers have already gotten hitched."

"Speak for yourself," Teagan quipped. "I'm still young and fresh. I could get a man if I wanted one. Right now, I just don't want to bother with it."

"Not even for the superhot, supremely talented man with the awesome curl pattern and the light eyes?" Nia winked.

"Least of all for him. I'm not about to risk my feelings on a musician. It's like I said. They just can't settle down, and I'm not about to be left heartbroken when he packs up his bass and hits that dusty trail."

Nia rolled her eyes. "It's a fling we're talking about here, girl. Not a game of *Oregon Trail*."

"Maybe so, but dating is way more dangerous. And I'm not fording that stream anytime soon." Shaking her head, Teagan turned her thoughts back to her still-wet toenails, and how she would spend the rest of her day off.

Because I'm not gonna spend it thinking about Maxton McCoy.

With a bowl of popcorn in hand, Maxton walked to his sofa. After setting the bowl on the table between the two glasses of iced cola there, he flopped down on the soft cushions. "What do you want to watch?"

Sharrod, seated next to him, glanced up from the screen of his phone. "It's Friday night, bro. To be honest, I'd rather hit the clubs and see if we can get into some trouble."

Rolling his eyes, Maxton grabbed the remote. "Fine. I'll choose."

"Why you ain't wanna go out this weekend?"

"We just came off tour, and I'm tired, Sharrod. Plus, since we about to start this new gig working with Lil Swagg, I think we need to tone it down. You know, rest up."

Sharrod scoffed. "We don't have the job yet, Max."

"Whatever, bro. I can play circles around those other bassists. I got this gig on lock, and so do you!" He slapped his friend on the back.

Sharrod shrugged in response. "I don't know, man. I feel like my cadence was off just slightly in that third and fourth bar."

"You're such a perfectionist." Flipping through the channels, he settled on a retro station that was playing reruns of the popular early nineties' competition show *American Gladiators*.

Looking up from his phone to the television screen, then at his friend, Sharrod said, "You're not seriously putting this on, are you?"

"Stop hating. This was my joint when I was little." He grinned as he watched Turbo, his favorite Gladiator, take on Laser in the joust. "Besides, I asked you what you wanted to watch, didn't I?"

"And I told you that I wanted to see some T & A out in those ATL streets." Sharrod clapped his hands together.

"Wow, man. Sometimes the San Bernardino Rico Suave really jumps out of your ass, doesn't it?" Maxton ribbed his old friend with his elbow.

"We can't all be from the hoity-toity hills of Calabasas, now, can we?" Sharrod punched him in the shoulder just as playfully.

Maxton stuck out his tongue. The two of them had been teasing each other like this ever since their days as roommates at University of Southern California's Thornton School of Music. They lived far enough apart that had they not gone to school together, they might never have met. "We may be from two different worlds, but we're both Trojans, bro."

"Fight on, Max."

"Fight on, Sharrod." He gave his friend a double fist bump.

He stared off toward the television but didn't seem to actually be watching the vintage goodness being played out on the screen. "Hey, you remember that night junior year, right after the homecoming game?"

"You mean that year we beat the Bruins by fourteen?"

He nodded. "Yeah, that game. Do you recall what we did after we won?"

Maxton scratched his head, searching through

his memory banks. "Oh, yeah! Wasn't that the time we went into the city to drink with some of the guys from the football team?"

"Hell, yeah. And we woke up the next morning, lying in the grass in the quad?"

"Shit, I'd forgotten about that. I don't remember much of the night after the game, but I do remember waking up when that cold water started hitting me. I was shirtless, you were missing your left shoe, and somebody had drawn mustaches on us with permanent markers." Thinking back, he could still feel the insistent chill of the water being thrown at his bare chest by the sprinklers and see the look of annoyance on the face of the groundskeeper as he'd stood over the two of them.

"To this day, I don't know if the sprinklers came on because they were on timer mode or because the landscape guy turned them on to wake us up." Sharrod shook his head with a laugh. "That shit was crazy. We were lucky, though. At least we didn't get tattooed like Ross Hamlin did."

Max burst out laughing. "I'd like to think he's gotten that photorealistic lobster lasered off by now."

"Me too. Who would hire him with that thing tattooed on his neck like that?"

"Crazy times, bro. Crazy, crazy times."

"You were like that all through school, man. Always hatching some scheme or dragging me along on some kind of adventure." Sharrod ran a hand over his close-cropped hair. "Sometimes I wonder how we even graduated."

Maxton shrugged. "That summer before senior year, my parents let me know that if I didn't straighten up and save some of my adventures for after I got my degree, they were going to cut me off. That sobered me right up." He took another swig of soda, thinking how he'd grown up in the years since his rowdy days at college. *Real life has certainly sobered me up, just like Mom and Pop did back in the day.* "I go for the sure thing now. That's why I'm glad you got us this audition with Lil Swagg."

"You really seem sure we got this gig, Max." Sharrod eyed him. "You stayed behind for a while after the auditions were over. Do you know something I don't?"

Maxton reached for his glass of cola and took a long drink.

Sharrod's brows furrowed. "Come on, now. What did you do, bribe somebody?"

"No, man." Maxton chuckled. "I'm telling you. We got the gig. Would you just trust me on this one?"

"If you say so." Sharrod shifted on his seat until he reclined against the sofa's plush backrest. "But that still doesn't tell me why you stayed behind for like twenty minutes after everybody else left."

Maxton scratched his chin, feeling the smile tugging at his lips. "I just had to stick around and talk to that fine-ass engineer."

"See? This is why I can't take your ass nowhere."

Sharrod gave him a sidelong glance. "You really used the audition as a pickup spot? And you had the nerve to give me grief for wanting to go to the club and pick up some honeys the old-fashioned way."

Maxton laughed as he grabbed a handful of popcorn. "Yeah, you say that now, but you saw her. You gotta admit she's fine as hell."

"Yeah, alright. I'll give you that. She's definitely easy on the eyes."

Remembering the brief glimpses he'd gotten of her beautiful face and shapely body, Max said, "I didn't go there with the intention of picking up anybody. We went there for a work opportunity. But once I saw her, man, I just couldn't resist. If nothing else, I had to at least know her name."

"I'm listening."

"I got to talk to her for a few minutes. Her name is unique… I've never heard it before."

"What is it?" Sharrod swiped across his phone's screen.

"Teagan. Anyway, she seems very serious about her work and very focused. She stayed after everybody had left, just to make sure her equipment was properly shut down."

"Mmm-hmm. Her name means 'little poet,' according to the internet."

He thought about the way her eyes sparkled and wondered if she had ever written any poetry. "Cool. Anyway, I know she doesn't play about that soundboard. She wouldn't let anybody else touch it. And aside from that, she's a twin. Her brother appeared just as I was starting to get some information out of her."

Sharrod drew back. "Oh, snap. Work obsessed, and with an evil twin?"

"I wouldn't call homeboy 'evil,' but he was definitely overprotective. I guess he's the older twin." Maxton stretched his arms above his head. "He was very concerned that I might be bothering his sister."

"Sounds like Miss Teagan might just be too much woman for you, bro. Better play it safe before she puts your heart in a headlock."

"You know what, Sharrod? I think I agree with you on this one."

Eyes wide, eyebrows raised, Sharrod said, "Come again?"

He ribbed him again. "Stop acting so surprised, I agree with you on occasion. And when it comes to Teagan, you're probably right. Shawty's thick and fine as hell. But I just can't get caught up in any romantic entanglements right now."

"I know I shouldn't question you agreeing with me, but I just gotta know why." Sharrod leaned forward, resting his chin on his hands.

"It's just that this is Atlanta. The cradle of southern hip-hop and R & B. If there's anywhere we're going to stumble on that next big gig, like an international tour, it's here." He rubbed his chin. "If I let this woman take over my heart and mind, how would I be able to focus on the next move in my career?"

"I see, I see. You actually making sense, bro." He chuckled. "Hard to believe from a dude that once locked himself on the balcony of our dorm room."

"Whatever man. I just gotta stay focused, plain and simple. I can't let an opportunity pass me by, not if I'm gonna save up enough to finally buy a house and put down roots somewhere."

"Do you think you'll go back to LA?"

He shook his head. "Hell, nah. I'm going somewhere where property prices are more advantageous, and they don't have wildfires every freakin' summer. Don't wanna deal with tornadoes, either." He watched absently as the credits rolled on television. "As much as I love playing bass, I don't wanna do it forever. I want a little piece of land and some peace and quiet."

"I hear you." Sharrod reached for the popcorn and scooped up the last handful. "Any more snacks, bro?"

"Yeah. There's some chips in the cabinet above the microwave."

As his friend walked off to refill the bowl, Maxton pushed all thoughts of Teagan and her overprotective brother out of his mind.

Four

Scooting her chair up to the workstation in Studio One, Teagan touched the screen to pull up the sound files from the recent auditions. Lil Swagg and his manager Rick were waiting on the sofa behind her, so she opened the folder as quickly as possible. "Okay, gentlemen. I'm going to play the audition tracks of the top two musicians in each category, as you requested."

"Sounds good," Swagg said, lifting his sunglasses from his eyes and placing them atop his head. "Let's hear it."

"Okay. We'll do bassists first." She started the audio file for bassist Allen Wright.

Swagg and Rick listened in silence, their expressions unreadable.

When the file finished, Swagg said, "You know, hearing that dude again, I don't really feel the vibe from him. Go ahead and play the other one."

Obliging him, Teagan opened Maxton's McCoy's sound file and pressed play. The room soon filled with the deep reverberations of his masterful playing, and she closed her eyes, remembering the look of bliss on his face as he worked the strings. His fingertips were deft and sure, and when he opened his eyes, his gaze had landed squarely on her face, causing a searing heat to rise from the pit of her stomach to the sides of her face.

The audio ended, and she looked to Swagg and Rick for their reactions.

Swagg's grin was as big as the diamond-studded letter *S* hanging from the gold chain around his neck. "Yeah, man. He's got the juice. That's my bassist."

Teagan nodded. "Noted. I'll let you hear the guitarists' audio next." She started the first file for that category. She continued on that way, opening and playing audio files until all eight had been heard. While Swagg and Rick deliberated, she leaned back in her chair and stared up at the recessed lighting above. What would it be like to come to the studio every day for the next few weeks, and see Maxton McCoy's impossibly handsome face with that devil-may-care smile? She inhaled deeply. If she were to remain the poised, professional ruler of this recording suite, she couldn't let him distract her from her duties.

I'd let Trevor take over, but Studio Two is booked solid until September. He won't have time to handle this suite, too. She sighed. Whenever Swagg and his manager decided to begin working on the album in earnest, there wouldn't be any good way to avoid the sexy bassist and his disarming swagger.

"Alright, Ms. Teagan, we've made our decision." Rick smiled in her direction. "Go ahead and take down these names for the liner notes. Maxton McCoy on bass, Brady Farmer on guitar, Sharrod Burton on drums and Mike Mendez on keyboard."

Teagan typed up the names in a text file. "Got it." Saving the text file in the folder with the audition audio, she asked, "When would you two like to start rehearsals for the album?" Silently, she prayed they'd say next week, to give her a few days to prepare herself for what was coming.

"Tomorrow," Swagg announced, standing from his seat. "I want to get this project done ASAP. Inspiration is flowing, and with a band this good, we should be done in no time. Then I can get back home to the BX."

"Homesick for New York already?" she asked.

"Yeah, I guess you could say that." Swagg grinned. "Nothin' like the Bronx, ya know? It's the cradle of hip-hop. You can draw a straight line from the pioneers like KRS-One and Boogie Down Productions, Melle Mel..."

Teagan nodded, picking up the list. "Afrika Bambaataa, T La Rock, Grandmaster Flash..."

"Hell, yeah! I love it when I meet a real hip-hop head." Swagg clapped his hands together. "Anyway, you can draw a line from those cats to Fat Joe and Terror Squad and Swizz Beatz to me." He closed his hands into fists, pointing both thumbs toward his chest. "The legacy continues, starting tomorrow, right here in this studio."

"See why I rock with this kid?" Rick gave Swagg a hearty slap on the back. "Let me call these dudes up and let 'em know."

While Rick made the calls, Teagan excused herself. "I'll be right back, gentlemen."

She walked down the corridor, turning off at the elevator bank and heading into the small snack bar just beyond it. There, she got herself a granola bar and a bottle of water from the vending machines to soothe her rumbling stomach. Tearing off the wrapper, she admonished herself. *No more skipping lunch, girl.*

She was standing just outside her recording suite, munching on the bar, when Rick and Swagg exited.

"Thanks for your help today," Swagg said, giving her a mock salute before tugging his shades over his eyes once again. "We'll see you at 10:00 a.m. sharp tomorrow."

Swallowing a mouthful of raisins and oats, she smiled and replied, "Sounds great. You two have a good evening."

"You do the same," Rick called over his shoulder as the two of them departed.

Alone in the hallway, Teagan devoured the rest of the granola bar, then twisted the cap on the water bottle. She'd just tipped it up when she heard someone call her name.

Peering around the corner, she saw her mother, Addison, strolling down the hall toward her. "Child, what are you doing snacking on your feet like that? Did you skip lunch again?"

"Hey, Mom." She gave her a sheepish grin. "I might have skipped it a little."

She pursed her lips. "Girl, either you did or you didn't, and we both know you did." Addison pinched her youngest child's cheek. "I don't know what I'm gonna do with you."

She held back the urge to roll her eyes, knowing her mother would pluck them right out of her head if she did. "I promise to do better with that. Now, what brings you down to the studio?"

"I came to see you." She eyed her daughter pointedly. "Did you pick out a dress or an outfit for the anniversary gala yet?"

She sighed. Her mother had been consumed with planning the studio's thirty-fifth-anniversary bash for what seemed like an eternity. "Mom, that party is still months away."

"I know. But if you end up getting something custom, like your sister and I did, you'll need that extra time for the designer and the seamstresses to get it done." Addison tucked a fallen curl back into her high bun. "So please, please decide what you're going to wear."

"I will. I promise." She tapped her chin, thinking. "Wait, what was the color scheme again?"

"It's purple and gold, Teagan." Addison's eyes flashed. "I can't believe you forgot that."

"I didn't, Mom. I was just kidding." She actually had forgotten, but this was her story and she was sticking to it.

Addison folded her arms over her chest. "Well, that little joke just earned you a personal escort to the family tailor, missy."

Teagan. "Oh, come on, Mom. You're not really going to…" She stopped, taking in the firm set of her mother's pursed lips. "Let me just run in the suite and get my purse."

"You do that," Addison insisted.

By the time Teagan returned with her purse, her mother's expression had relaxed. "Mom, I'm gonna guess you're not doing this to the boys."

Addison shook her head. "No. It takes no time to have a suit tailored, but making something custom is a whole different matter." She started down the hallway toward reception. "Let's go."

Teagan used her keys to lock up the recording suite, then followed her mother outside. In the parking lot, they climbed into Addison's midsize royal blue SUV.

While they drove, Teagan leaned back against the

passenger headrest, watching the familiar scenery whizz by.

"What's the matter, honey? You seem distracted."

"It's nothing, Mom." She blew out a breath. "Lil Swagg has chosen his band, and he wants to start working on his album tomorrow."

"That's good news." Addison flicked the wheel to make a right turn. "He's paid for studio time for the next several weeks, so he may as well use it."

"That's true." She kept her gaze out the window, not wanting to look in her mother's direction. *If she sees my face, it will give me away.* "I guess I'm just…a little nervous. It's an ambitious project, and I want things to turn out just right for Swagg. I don't want anything to interfere with getting him the results he's after."

"That makes sense, but it sounds like you're doubting your ability to deliver on this album." Addison stopped at a red light and turned her way. "Teagan, you have to know by now that there isn't a better sound engineer in town. Whatever an artist throws at you, you can handle it."

"You sound so sure."

"That's because I am." Addison winked, then accelerated as the light changed green. "Don't you spend one more minute thinking about what might go wrong. Everyone in that room tomorrow will be there because they earned their space there through talent, and that includes you."

"Thanks, Mom." She smiled, accepting the wisdom of her mother's words.

Come tomorrow, I'm bringing my A-game.

When Maxton walked into Studio One at nine fifty on Tuesday morning, he resisted the urge to linger near Teagan and crossed the outer suite to the sofa. There, Lil Swagg, dressed in baggy jeans, a green polo and matching baseball cap, and an enormous gold chain featuring a yellow diamond-encrusted dollar sign, sat next to Rick, who was similarly dressed, minus the hardware. "Good morning. Thank you again, guys, for the opportunity."

Swagg grinned from behind his dark sunglasses. "No problem, homie. Just go in there and kill."

"You got it." He shook hands with the two men and returned to the soundboard, where he smiled in Teagan's direction. "Good morning, Teagan." He paused, letting his eyes delight in her appearance. Today, she wore a sleeveless orange silk blouse with a navy pencil skirt. Small polished-gold hoops sparkled in her ears. The outfit, along with the thin gold chains around her neck and wrists, accentuated her toned arms and long, shapely legs. Lowering his voice a bit, he said, "Told you we'd be working together."

"Morning, Maxton. And yes, I think I recall you saying that." She flexed her ankle as she crossed one leg over the other, showcasing her stylish orange-

and-gold, color-blocked pumps. Giving him a quick nod, she let her glossy lips form a ghost of a smile.

Sharrod, who was right behind him, chuckled. "Let's keep the line moving, bro. You got three dudes and their equipment behind you."

Maxton rolled his eyes. "Please. You're carrying two wooden sticks."

"Four," Sharrod corrected. "I brought two pairs of sticks, just in case."

"Whatever, man." Reluctantly, he moved past Teagan at the workstation, passing through the open door into the booth.

The booth was set for recording, with two amps on either side of the space. There were two tricked-out drum sets positioned next to each other, one Tama Starclassic Performer acoustic set and one Roland V electronic set, both in rich black with pearl-and-silver detailing. He could easily identify both sets after years of knowing Sharrod. There were also five stools positioned around the space, one of which was stationed near the mic and headphones that Swagg would use to lay down his verses.

Carefully maneuvering his instrument around the various items in the room, he started setting up by removing his bass from the carrying case and connecting the cable to the amp he'd used during his audition, the one to the far left. Then he took a seat on the stool next to it.

Sharrod seated himself on the low stool behind

the acoustic drum set while the keyboardist and guitarists made their preparations as well.

Swagg entered the booth then. "Y'all ready to
do this?"

Maxton and the other musicians all responded
affirmatively.

"Cool. Let's make sure you all know each other's
names. You gonna be spending a lot of time together."

As the introductions were made, Maxton learned
the names of the keyboardist, Mike, and the guitarist, Brady.

"Alright, now that we got that outta the way, let
me run down my goals." Swagg clapped his hands
together. "This album is eleven tracks, and I want to
have it done in sixty days or less. I know that sounds
like a lot. But before I left NYC, I worked with Chanel the Titan to produce eleven stripped-down beats.
We'll use those as a basis and flesh them out into
full-fledged songs."

Maxton nodded. "I see. We're just bringing the
tracks to life, then."

"Right, my dude." Swagg pointed his direction.
"The work is already started. Now we're gonna finish it."

Rick entered then, handing them each a slip the
size of an index card. "These are the tracks we'll
be recording. As we move through them, lean into
your artistry. Feel free to improvise and add a little

spice wherever you think it's needed. That's why we hired you."

"Now the engineer will talk with y'all for a minute, then we'll get started," Swagg said as he and Rick left the booth.

Glancing at the card, Maxton eased over to Sharrod. "See the name of the fifth track?"

"Yeah. Very colorful." Sharrod chuckled.

Most of the tracks had ambiguous or even undecided titles. But track five, called "Eff Money J," had a pretty transparent purpose. "Ever worked on a diss record before?"

Sharrod shook his head. "Nah, but first time for everything, I guess."

Teagan entered then, holding a tablet close to her chest, and Maxton couldn't help staring at her legs as she walked.

"Okay, gentlemen. Swagg has generously added a bonus to your payment due to the tight turnaround he's asking for on this album. You should already have received an email from me detailing the terms, the compensation for the sessions tied to this project and the royalties going forward. Are there any questions or concerns about that?"

No one had any, and Maxton surmised that was because they were making about 20 percent over the typical fee for album work plus a pretty fair royalty on the finished project. Even if Swagg worked them for twelve hours a day for the whole month, Maxton knew the compensation would still be fair.

"Great. I'm going to pass my tablet around, and if each of you would sign and date by your names, to indicate that you're good with all the terms, we can go ahead and get started."

They passed around the device and the sleek black stylus, then Maxton handed it back to Teagan.

Their hands momentarily brushed during the exchange, and he felt a twinge go through him. Her skin was so soft and warm against his that his brain short-circuited for a beat.

"Maxton, are you going to let go?"

Realizing he was still gripping the stylus, he released it into her hand. "Sorry about that. Just checked out for a minute."

"Try not to do that while we're recording." Her tone light and teasing, she took the stylus, turned and walked away, returning to her workstation in the outer suite.

He swallowed. When his gaze shifted to Sharrod, he saw his friend sitting behind the drum set, shaking his head. The other two musicians were surreptitiously watching as well, and Mike, the keyboardist, wasn't even doing a good job of hiding it.

Maxton cringed. *Guess I gotta be a little less obvious about my fascination with our illustrious sound engineer.*

The session got underway with Teagan first playing a track, then allowing the musicians to improvise accompanying music. They spent the better part of the day working on the first track, and by noon, Swagg was satisfied enough to lay down his chorus over the music.

They continued working on the song until just after two when Swagg took off the headphones and set them on the hook. Raising his hand above his head, he said, "Alright, y'all. Take a lunch. My stomach 'bout to collapse."

Chuckling, Maxton propped his bass in the stand behind his amp and headed with Sharrod toward the door.

In the hallway, Sharrod asked, "Where do you wanna eat?"

Maxton shrugged. "I could go for a burger and fries, but I'm not picky about where we get it."

Teagan exited the recording suite and walked by them carrying an insulated lunch bag. She nodded to them as she passed and disappeared through the rear door.

Maxton started walking in that direction.

Sharrod said, "You really following shorty?"

"Not really. We parked on the side, so this door's closer, remember?"

Rolling his eyes, Sharrod said, "Whatever. I'll meet you in the car. Don't spend our whole lunch break mackin', either."

"It won't take but a minute."

They exited, and Sharrod went right, toward the parking lot, while Maxton went left, toward the courtyard behind the building. There, Teagan sat on a bench, using a plastic fork to eat from a clear container.

Walking up to her, he said, "Looks good. What is it?"

She held her hand over her mouth as she finished chewing, then swallowed. "Just some leftover chicken alfredo I made last night."

"You always bring lunch?"

She shook her head. "To be honest, I usually skip it. But my Mom ain't having that, so I'm trying to get better about it."

"Your mom. You mean, Addison Woodson, right?"

She nodded. "Yes. 404 Sound is a family-owned business, has been for over thirty years. All my siblings work upstairs in the c-suites."

"Including your overzealous twin?"

"Yeah. Don't mind Miles. He can't help himself."

"He wants to make sure you're good. I can respect that." An image of his own sister came to mind, but he didn't want to talk about her for fear of dredging up that same old pain that had become his constant companion these last eight months. "Seems like the Woodsons really look out for each other."

"We do." She set down her fork, gesturing toward the parking lot. "Your friend looks a little agitated."

Maxton glanced that way to see Sharrod flagging him down, air-traffic-controller-style, from the far end of the parking lot. Shaking his head, he said,

"Yeah, let me go. We do need to eat before we go back in session. See you later."

"Later." She raised her hand, giving him a small wave as he walked away.

Five

"Come on, Teagan. Keep up."

"Sheesh, I'm coming." Teagan picked up her pace to keep up with her twin brother's long strides. "You know, you could also slow down a bit. Not all of us are triathletes."

Miles chuckled. "Sis, I can see why you kept blowing me off, or agreeing and then flaking on me, all these months. You're out of shape."

She stuck out her tongue. "Shut up, Miles, before I bop you."

"You gotta catch up to me first." He laughed and sped up to a jog.

"Ugh." She picked up her pace again, thankful that the path was paved. They were making their way down Proctor Creek Greenway, a two-lane walking trail in the northeastern part of the city. It was closer to work than Piedmont Park, so she'd taken that into consideration when she finally agreed to come with her brother on one of his weekly fitness walks.

As she dashed along on the right side of the broken yellow line separating the lanes, she took in the scenery. The scorching heat of the July day was finally beginning to wane, and the sun was sinking lower on its trip toward the horizon.

The greenway, which had only opened in the last few years, was certainly not the most pristine or scenic of them all. It wasn't anywhere near as manicured as Piedmont Park's trails. That was largely due to its location in an old industrial area of town. The grassy expanse along the path was dotted with the ruins of many aged factories, warehouses and the like. Towering overhead were the silvery-white poles of power lines, which, while providing vital electricity to the city's ever-expanding power grid, did nothing to add to the scenery.

Still, the trail had its own, unique brand of urban beauty. The winding path took them through deep wooded groves where kudzu and English ivy climbed the hilly banks of the creek, rising up to shroud the trunks and branches of the willow trees. The water, somehow both murky and clear at the same time, babbled as it flowed over the rocky creek floor toward the Chattahoochee River.

Finally, mercifully, she came abreast of her

brother, and as she'd promised, used her open hand to pop the back of his head.

"Well, look at that. You finally caught up!"

"I can do anything with proper motivation," she quipped. "And nothing pleases me more than going upside your big head."

He laughed. "Whatever works, I guess." He blew out a breath and slowed his pace a bit. "Alright, we can ease up now. We're already about a mile in."

"Meanwhile, have I mentioned how much you resemble a highlighter today, Miles?"

He glanced down at his electric green T-shirt and running shorts. "No, but I appreciate the feedback." He eyed her. "By the way, you look like a housewife on a run to the warehouse store."

"Whatever." She'd chosen her fuchsia tank and purple cotton shorts for comfort, not fashion. "It's too hot to think too hard about what I'm wearing. I just tossed this into my bag before I left the house this morning so I could come out here with you." She adjusted the hook-and-loop closure at the back of her visor, which kept threatening to undo the low ponytail she'd slapped her hair into. "And now that I have, it's my supreme hope that you will stop inviting me."

"Nah, sis. I need you healthy, just as healthy as me." He reached over and squeezed her cheek. "That way I can pester you well into our nineties."

"Sounds delightful," she said with mock disgust.

A breeze blew through, rustling the leaves of the trees and providing momentary relief from the oppressive humidity. "Don't worry. About this time of year, I take my walks indoors, because it gets too hot to be out here for very long."

"That's a relief." The temperatures had fallen off since noon but were still in the low eighties, even as sunset approached. "Because I'm not doing this again unless it's in an air-conditioned location."

"Gotcha." Miles lifted his baseball cap, using the small towel he'd had slung over his shoulder to mop his brow. "I love coming out into nature. I need this break from the finance department. Do you know that we were the last department to turn in our quarterly reports?"

She shook her head. "Nia mentioned that somebody was late, but she didn't say who."

"Ugh. I was so annoyed. But my best accountant just had a baby, and things have really been backed up since she left on maternity leave." He sighed. "I had to lean on my other three staff accountants to pick up the pace, just for us to still be late. But at least we showed a rise in profits since the first quarter. I think it could have been a bigger gain if we just…"

"Miles, hush. Didn't we just go over all this at that 7:00 a.m. meeting this morning? I don't want to rehash it, even though I wasn't caffeinated enough to process most of it."

"Yeah, you're right. Tell me about what's going on in the studio. How are things going with Swagg's album?" He sounded genuinely interested.

"That's still shop talk, but I'll indulge you. I think things are going well, for the most part."

"What's the hang-up, then?"

"Today, we recorded the second track six times because the bassist couldn't decide on an interpretation to stick to."

"The bassist keeps tempo for everybody else, so I can see how that would be annoying." He scratched his chin. "The bassist, huh? That wouldn't be the guy in the leather jacket that I saw sniffing around you last week, would it?"

She stared. "How do you know that?"

He shrugged. "Word gets around the 404 building pretty fast. His name's Something McCoy, right?"

"Maxton McCoy." She blew out a breath. "And yes, he's the bassist Swagg chose. Anyway, Swagg ended up choosing the second version out of the six we tried, so it seems to me that we went on with the improvisation for far too long."

"Maybe a little."

"I mean, Swagg wants this album done in less than two months, and I don't want to miss the deadline because we're dawdling in the studio, you know?"

"Makes sense to me." Miles stopped as they reached the crosswalk at Johnson Road, turning toward his sister and grasping her shoulders gently. "I'm going to ask you this again. Is he bothering you? Because if he is, I'm happy to make him eat some sheet music or something."

She laughed. "No, he's not bothering me, Miles. This is just par for the course, a part of the creative process. While it's frustrating, it's not a problem." She grabbed his hat brim and tugged it down. "And if you're worried about us getting together, don't be. If he can't even make up his mind well enough to settle on a bassline, he probably isn't the settling-down type."

"I'm glad you can see that."

"Why must you always resort to threats of violence, anyway? You've been that way since we were kids."

He readjusted his hat. "Probably because I'm serious. You're my twin, so if somebody hurts you, they're essentially hurting me, too." He gave her shoulders a squeeze. "Frankly, sis, I'm not having that."

"I appreciate that, chucklehead." She leaned up and gave him a peck on the cheek.

They crossed the two-lane road, continuing down the trail on the other side. "Are we almost at the end?"

He nodded. "Yeah. It's not much farther to Sanford Road, and once we get there, we can take the MARTA back to the building to get our cars."

"Great, because I'm exhausted." She could feel the sweat rolling down her back but decided not to share that little detail with her brother. "I feel like I should get to eat pizza after this. I'm sure I already burned it off."

"Throw some veggies on it and I'll allow it," Miles replied.

"Fair enough."

They finished the rest of the trail in silence, then took the Green Line back to 404 headquarters. As Teagan trudged to her car, sweaty, tired and hungry, she heard her brother call her name. "What, Miles? And make it quick, because I'm starving and you're the only thing standing between me and a hot pizza."

He laughed. "I just wanted to say, thanks for coming on the walk with me, grumpy. I know you hate working out, but walking is a good way to ease into it."

"I suppose. I just hope your indoor trail is much shorter."

"It will be. Hard to cram three miles inside a building." He tapped his chin as if thinking. "Although, if we did enough laps, we could still make three miles…"

She pursed her lips. "Bye, Miles."

"Bye, sis. Love you," he called as he marched off toward his jet-black pickup.

"Love you, too." She opened the driver's-side door of her white coupe and climbed inside. As soon as she started the engine, she cranked the air conditioner as high as it would go. Snatching off her visor, she looked in the rearview and shook her head at the sight of the curls plastered to her sweaty brow. "Dang. I definitely gotta wash my hair." Wash day was an ordeal she was too tired to carry out, so she resolved to do it tonight but sleep in her turban and deal with the detangling in the morning.

After taking a few moments to let her body temperature drop enough for her to focus on the road, she backed out of her parking space and headed for home.

Maxton sat on one of the tall leather stools at the bar inside Rogue Sports Pub, his eyes glued to the television. The anchors on SportsCenter were busy bantering about the latest baseball matchup between Atlanta's hometown team and the team from Miami.

"Yo, Maxton."

He turned to his left, his attention drawn away from the commentary. "What's up, Sharrod?"

"Are we gonna order? Or are you gonna just keep staring at the TV?"

The bartender, Nick, stood nearby, rubbing a drying cloth over the glass in his hand. "You ready to order, playa? You've had my menu for like twenty minutes. Besides, weren't y'all in here last week?" He set the glass down in the rack, then pulled out his pen and pad from his apron pocket.

Maxton chuckled. "Yeah, my bad. Anyway, let me just get the chicken nachos and a glass of Lee's finest."

"And I'll have the same. Just make my nachos with steak, please."

"You got it." Nick took their menus and slipped them into the holder on the far end of the counter.

Then he disappeared behind the bar to deliver their order slip to the kitchen.

Maxton let his gaze sweep over the interior as the sports show went to a commercial break. The brick-red walls were covered with pennants, posters, jerseys and other collectible items representing the four main professional teams that called Atlanta home: baseball, football, and men's and women's basketball. Neon signs advertising popular beers and the occasional photograph of some famous athlete who'd stopped in for a bite to eat punctuated the collection of memorabilia.

"You've been unfocused all day today, bro." Sharrod poked him in the shoulder with his index finger. "What's up with you?"

"What makes you say that?"

"Oh, please. Did we not have to slog through six takes of one song, just because you couldn't settle on a bass line?" He stared. "I'm sure I'm not the only one who noticed, my dude."

Maxton sighed. "Fair enough. I was a little distracted today."

"And I bet I know why, since you spent the entire session staring at the sound engineer." He stared, then gave him the slow blink.

"You have to know her name is Teagan by now."

"I know her name. You sure as hell mention it enough." Rolling his eyes, he drummed his fingertips on the bar.

Maxton tilted his head to one side. "Stop hating.

Either way, she can't be blamed for how distracted I was today. Not all of it."

Sharrod scoffed. "She can't be blamed for any of it. How is it her fault you can't stop staring at her like you're the bear and she's the pot of honey?"

Maxton frowned. *Why is Sharrod making such a big deal about this?* "Anyway, that song is really special. Because of the subject matter, it required a lot more thought to determine the best interpretation."

"I guess," Sharrod said with a shrug.

"Come on, man. Have you really listened to the lyrics? That song is all about the pain of losing someone close to you. I don't know what they used for you drummers, but that's the song I was asked to play along with for my audition."

"Nah, today was the first time I heard that track." Sharrod tapped his chin. "But if you heard it before, why didn't you feel confident about how to work with it?"

"It's pretty heavy material, man. I just wanted to do it justice. There's a lot of pain in that song, and I wanted to make sure I conveyed it while still keeping true to the overall tone of the album."

"Here you go, guys." Nick slid them their beers.

"Thanks," Sharrod said as he gripped the handle of his mug. "I can see that. I know it's important to get the vibe right. It's just that you seemed like you were floundering there for a minute. I've never really seen you lose your cool like that."

He ran a hand over his hair. There was a certain

cluelessness in his friend's words, a sign that he was still blissfully unaware of the full measure of pain Maxton had suffered when he lost Whitney. And since he'd never let himself fully vent that pain to his closest friend, he supposed he had only himself to blame. "I didn't know it was that bad from the outside. But I'll be on my toes from now on. Promise."

"Good, because we've still got nine more tracks." Sharrod raised his mug.

Maxton grabbed his own and took a long drink. The citrusy flavor of the Rogue's signature IPA invaded his taste buds, carrying with it the hints of vanilla and the spicy cinnamon that gave the beer its bite.

"Listen. Do you remember when we were on tour with BJ the Chicago Kid, and I missed the last show?"

"Yeah, of course I do," Maxton replied. "They had to replace you with a damn drum machine at the last minute."

"I know." Sharrod shook his head. "And I'm ashamed of that, believe me. Did I ever tell you why I didn't show up that night?"

Their nachos arrived, just in time for the story. Maxton reached for a chip laden with grilled chicken, cheese sauce and jalapeños. "No, you didn't. So what happened?"

"I got caught up with one of the groupies. There were these two girls who had been following BJ's tour bus for the last three stops. I'd seen them hanging around the venues, and I just assumed they were BJ stans. But that night when he did his final stop in his home city, I found out that one of them was only interested in 'the hot drummer.'" He made air quotes around the last three words.

"Oh, boy." Maxton shook his head. "Go on."

"Anyway, I was hanging out behind the theater before the show. Me and a couple of the roadies were just chilling, trading war stories. We'd already moved the equipment onstage, so there really wasn't anything left to do, and it was still, like, two hours before showtime. The two girls come twisting across the parking lot. I mean these girls are looking for something, and the shorter one was just bold about it. She walks right up to me and says, real sultry, 'What are you getting into tonight, drummer boy?'"

Maxton crunched on another chip, nodding. Sharrod's stories were always wild, and though he was never sure if they were fully true, that didn't diminish the entertainment factor.

"So now the roadies are laughing and joking while she's introducing herself. Said her name was Candy. But this girl was thick, with this cute little leather dress on. She had the boom and the pow, you know what I mean?"

"Yeah, I get it," Maxton said. "Go on."

"So I was like, 'Hopefully, I'm getting into you.' Well, after I said that, it was on. We left, got a rideshare over to a hotel a few blocks down the street and that girl spent the rest of the night turning me inside out." He rubbed his hands together. "Shorty showed me some new things, that's for damn sure."

Maxton chuckled around a mouthful of food.

"When I woke up the next morning, she was gone. No note, none of that. Looking back, I'm lucky she didn't take my wallet while I was asleep." He shook his head. "I called up BJ's people, and they were understandably pissed. I had to reimburse them what they paid me for the missed show."

"Dude. Why are you telling me this now?"

"Because there's a lesson in there, man. I screwed myself over by letting a pretty girl distract me from work. And if you ever get the call to go back out on tour with BJ, I can't go, because they banned me from touring with him. Permanently."

Maxton winced. "Ouch. I didn't know you got blacklisted."

"Yeah, I did. I missed out on touring with Only the Family and Lil Durk because of it. Apparently, Chicago dudes are comparing notes and whatnot." With a solemn shake of his head, Sharrod dug into his nachos. "Messed up my money for the honey. Bad move."

While he continued eating his own food, Maxton thought about Sharrod's rather crazy story. He was right. He was lucky "Candy" hadn't robbed him blind; that probably wasn't even her real name. Sharrod had taken an extraordinarily dumb risk to get in a girl's panties, and even though he hadn't gotten jacked, he hadn't escaped unscathed, either. "Please tell me you'll never do that shit again. What if she had bad intentions? We could have found your ass dead in a ditch somewhere."

"You don't have to tell me, and no, I won't be doing anything that stupid ever again." He took a drink. "I know it's an extreme example, but you should still take it as a cautionary tale. Don't let a pretty face keep you from meeting your professional goals."

Maxton nodded but didn't respond. Finishing up the last of his nachos, he pushed the plate away before draining his beer. "Hey, Nick, can I get another?"

While the bartender refilled his mug with the golden brew, he thought about his recent promise to Sharrod. His friend's crazy-bananas story had served as a firm reminder that he should stick to his goals, not to Teagan.

That might be easier said than done, but he had to at least try.

Six

Passing by the reception desk Thursday evening, Teagan could see that Barbara had already gone home for the evening. Glancing at her phone, she checked the time. It was twenty minutes past six, well past business hours. But it had still been a short day in the studio compared to the previous day. The band had invited her out for pizza with them, but she'd stayed behind to get things ready for tomorrow's session.

She swung open the glass-paneled door and stepped outside. The oppressive heat and humidity of the Georgia summer greeted her, and she groaned. Even with the lightweight fabric of the knee-length sage-green sundress she'd worn into work, there was no escape from the oven-like atmosphere. She picked up her pace as she walked to her car, anticipating the glorious relief of air-conditioning waiting inside the cabin.

She sniffed, inhaling the familiar, unwelcome aroma of cigarette smoke, and cringed. Unlocking the driver's-side door of her car, she reached for the handle and stopped short when someone called her name.

Turning toward the sound, she saw her father's personal secretary jogging toward her. She wore her typical work attire of a black button-down shirt and matching slacks with low-heeled pumps. She pinched the filter of a lit cigarette between her fingers. *That explains the smell.*

"Teagan, hold on a minute." Gloria stopped on the sidewalk in front of her.

"Hey, Gloria, haven't seen you in a while." She couldn't help noticing the way the older woman's voice wavered.

"So, how was your day today? Is everything good in the studio?"

"Everything's fine. I think we're making good progress on Lil Swagg's album."

"That's good to hear." Her head bobbed with approval.

She eyed Gloria for a moment, then asked the question lingering on the tip of her tongue. "You're... smoking again?"

Her gaze skittered around, and she let out a humorless chuckle. "Haven't smoked in months. It's my nerves, you know. When they get frayed, I slip up."

Teagan frowned. "Is everything alright? What's going on that's made you pick up smoking again?"

She nibbled her bottom lip before turning away to take another pull. With her back turned, she blew the smoke toward the building before facing her again. "You're about to find out. It's the whole reason I stopped you." Reaching into the back pocket of her slacks, Gloria handed her a folded, bright white square.

"What's this?" Teagan opened it up and saw that it was an envelope, addressed to her father. There was no return address.

"I...think it's better if you just look at it." Gloria shifted her weight from left to right, then back again. "You know your father asked me to start screening his mail years ago, back when he was still CEO. To cut down on wasted time, I read his mail and only bring him the important stuff. And doing that for him has never been a problem for me." She shook her head solemnly. "Until today."

Teagan shifted her focus from Gloria's drawn face to the unremarkable-looking envelope in her hand. Taking a deep breath, she extracted the folded letter and opened it, reading aloud. "Dear Mr. Woodson..." She stopped speaking the words but kept reading through the first four sentences. Her heart climbed into her throat like a squirrel charging up a tree. "Holy shit."

"Yeah, that's about the same reaction I had when I read it over my lunch break. I've been trying to figure out what to do since then." Gloria tossed the cigarette on the sidewalk and twisted the sole of her shoe over it. "So, I'm gonna go and leave this to you." She turned away.

"Wait a minute." Teagan touched her arm. "Why me? You screen his mail for a reason. Why didn't you give this to him? It obviously falls in the 'important' category."

"I can't, Teagan. I can't take this to him." Gloria's lips twisted into a sad frown. "I've known him for years. And the best way to soften bad news is to get it from his baby girl." She stepped back. "Please, do this for me, as a favor."

Seeing the discomfort written all over Gloria's expression and her slumped shoulders, Teagan slowly nodded. "Fine. But I think you're putting too much faith in this making the news any easier to take."

"Thank you." She spun and speed-walked to her small sedan. Within the next few minutes, she'd peeled out of the parking lot.

Guess she didn't want to give me a chance to change my mind. With the letter in hand, Teagan locked her car and reentered the building with her key card. Taking the elevator up to the fourth floor, she walked past her unused office. Her parents gave her an office, just like the rest of her siblings, but she preferred to spend all of her time in the studio.

She continued down to the end of the corridor and entered her father's office.

Caleb Woodson was seated behind his big oak desk, talking on the phone. Wearing a dove-gray suit with a charcoal-gray shirt and pocket square, he looked every bit the old Southern gentleman she'd always thought he was. His short black curls were gray around the temples, and a full, salt-and-pepper beard surrounded his smiling mouth.

He glanced up when she entered, gesturing her to the chair across from him.

She watched him while he finished his conversation, thinking of the way his deep skin tone had mixed with her mother's fairer one to produce the medium tones that she and all her siblings had. Or so she'd assumed. The longer she stared at him, the more aware she became of just how awkward things were about to get.

He finally ended the call, replacing the handset in the cradle. "Hey, sweetheart. To what do I owe the pleasure of this visit from my little princess?"

She gave him a half smile. "Come on, Dad. I'm a long way from my castle playhouse at this point."

"Maybe so, but I'll always see you that way." He winked. "So, what do you need?"

"Can I ask you something?"

"Sure, honey." He settled back in his chair, tenting his fingers.

She paused, thinking of how best to phrase her

question. "Did you…ever have any other serious relationships? You know, before Mom?"

He shrugged. "Sure, I suppose. I mean, I had a couple of long-term girlfriends, but I've never proposed to anyone else but Addy." He gave her a sidelong glance. "Wait a minute. What brought on this newfound curiosity about my past?"

Looking into her father's eyes, she searched for any inkling that what she'd read in the letter might be true. Could this really be happening? Now that she was past the initial shock, her mind was free to process the further implications of this whole situation. Was it possible that the man she'd loved and looked up to her whole life wasn't the man she thought he was? Knowing she wouldn't find the answer any other way, she resolved to cut to the chase. She drew a deep breath. "Gloria asked me to…well… I have something to give you."

His brows scrunched together. He extended his hand. "Alright."

Handing over the letter, she rested her hands in her lap and waited.

In the silence, she could hear the moment he reached the second sentence. His breath grew louder, more erratic. Watching his face, she saw his nostrils flare and his eyes flash. Moments later, he forcefully pushed back from his desk and jumped to his feet. "What the hell is this?"

She swallowed. "It's a letter. It came for you today, and Gloria wanted me to give it to you…"

He read aloud, "Dear Mr. Woodson, my name is Keegan Woodbine and I have reason to believe you are my biological father." He balled up the paper and tossed it into the wastebasket. "This is absolute bullshit."

"I told Gloria that having me bring this to you wouldn't make it any easier to hear." Teagan ran her hand over her hair. "I'm sorry I upset you, Dad."

He shook his head. "This isn't your fault and I won't have you taking any blame for it. It's not Gloria's fault, either." He touched his fingertips to his temples. "There's no way this is possible. I've loved your mother for most of my life, and I've never got any other woman pregnant." He looked at his daughter, his eyes pleading. "You have to believe me, baby girl. Please say you believe me."

She nodded slowly in response to his earnest declaration. "Yes, Dad. I believe you."

He laid his hand over his chest. "Good. I'm relieved to hear that."

"There's still the matter of this accusation, though. How are you going to handle this? What are you going to tell Mom?"

He gestured to the wastebasket. "You just saw me handle it. That letter was nothing but lies, and there's nothing further to do. And I'm certainly not going to needlessly upset your mother by telling her about this."

She balked. "Dad. If this person went to the trouble of sending that letter, do you really think they won't pursue this claim further?"

"It isn't true!" He slapped his hand on his desk.

"Regardless of that, I don't think they're going to just let it go. What happens when they send another letter? Or escalate this thing somehow?"

His shoulders slumped, he turned toward the window behind his desk and opened the blinds. "Teagan, I already told you. It's all lies, and I don't want to hear another word about it." He stuffed his hands into the hip pockets of his slacks.

She'd come face-to-face with her father's famous stubborn streak, but she still tried to make him see reason. "But Dad…"

"Young lady, if you 'but Dad' me one more time, we're going to have a problem." He kept his back turned to her as he spoke. "It's late, Teagan. Go home and get yourself some dinner."

She knew a dismissal when she heard it. Rising from her seat, she stood and walked out of the room.

Maxton slung the strap of his bass's carrying case over his shoulder and followed Sharrod from the courtyard behind 404 to the front parking lot. "You know what? Mike and Brady are actually fun guys. I'm glad we went for a pizza with them after the session."

Sharrod nodded. "Yeah, they seem like good dudes." He scratched his chin as they rounded the corner to the front of the building. "Hey, isn't that Teagan over there?" He pointed.

Maxton's gaze followed the gesture. There she was, sitting in the driver's seat of her little white coupe. "Yeah, man. That's her. What is she doing there alone?"

They walked closer, and the picture of her became clearer. She was reclining there, her thick curls against the headrest, looking straight ahead. As they approached from the passenger side, he could see the tears streaming down her face.

"Oh, snap. She's crying," Sharrod said.

Maxton slid the strap of his bass off his shoulder.

"Let me guess," Sharrod said, tucking his drumsticks into the back pocket of his cargo shorts. "You want me to take this so you can run to her rescue, right?"

Handing over his instrument, he nodded. "Call me crazy, but I can't just leave her here like this, man."

Sharrod took the bass. "I'll leave it in the trunk for tomorrow's session, then. And how are you getting home?"

He shrugged. "I'll take the train if I need to. Just be at my place at the regular time tomorrow to pick me up, and we're good." He kept his eyes on Teagan as he spoke.

"No romantic entanglements, my ass." Sharrod snickered as he walked away toward his rental.

She finally noticed his presence, and her eyes slid shut.

Maxton walked around to the driver's side of the car. He tapped gently on her window with his knuckle.

Her eyes popped open, and she swiped her hand over her face before rolling the window down. "Hey, Maxton, what's up?"

"That's what I came to ask you." He watched her intently. "What's wrong?"

"Nothing." She shook her head, wiping away more tears. "I'm fine."

"You're sitting alone in your car, crying, so we both know that isn't true."

She cringed, and he couldn't tell if the change in her expression was brought on by embarrassment, annoyance or both.

"Listen, I'm not trying to get in your business or anything like that." Maxton crouched so they could be at eye level. "But I am concerned that you seem so upset. Do you maybe wanna talk about it?"

She sniffled. "Do you want to listen?"

He nodded. "I do."

She jerked her head toward the passenger seat. "Get in. Just watch out for my purse."

He did as she asked, carefully avoiding her bag as he joined her in the car. After he buckled up, she pulled out of the lot. Before he had a chance to ask where they were headed, she spoke.

"There's a coffee shop right around the corner. We can go there."

"Sounds good."

As they drove, she took several deep breaths and, from what he could tell, composed herself. The tears were no longer flowing, but the sadness remained in her eyes.

Soon, they pulled into the parking lot of a small, one-story building with a glass door and plenty of windows along the front. He read the sign affixed to the roofline and smiled. "The Bodacious Bean? What a name."

"It's family-owned, and it's been here for decades." She cut the engine and undid her belt. "Best lattes in the city." Grabbing her bucket-style black bag from the floorboard, she opened her door.

"It's been a long day. I could use a little pick-me-up."

He walked behind her and couldn't help observing the sway of her hips in the short green sundress she wore and the way her calves flexed as she walked in her high-heeled sandals. They entered the place to the sound of a tinkling bell. Maxton inhaled, and the rich aroma of the coffee awakened his senses. "Damn. It smells amazing in here."

"They use their own crossbred bean. Can't get this stuff anywhere else." She approached the counter with all the confidence of a regular and greeted the barista. "Hi. Can I please get a medium iced–caramel latte?" She started fishing around in her purse, probably for her wallet.

Maxton sidled up next to her. "I'll have what she's having. And add a couple of croissants, please." He waved his credit card over the contactless processing machine and paid before she could.

"You didn't have to do that." She eyed him as she dropped her wallet back into her bag.

"I know." He shrugged. "But it's not a problem, really."

She observed him for a few silent beats. "Let's get a table."

He followed her to a two-top in the back, positioned beneath the last window along the coffee shop's eastern wall. He pulled out the chair facing the windows, and after she sat down, he took the seat across from her.

They watched each other quietly for a few moments.

"Whenever you're ready to talk," he assured, "I'm ready to listen." The barista called out their order, and he stood. "I'll grab it. One sec." He returned with a small tray holding their order and set it down. "Here you go." He slid one tall glass, a straw and one ceramic plate her way.

"Thanks." She opened the black straw, stuck it in the glass and took a long sip through it. "It's been a hell of a day."

"How so?"

"Everything was pretty normal until I was on my way home. My father's secretary stopped me as I was getting into my car, and from that moment on, my day turned to a pile of crap."

"Yikes." He drank some of his latte and found it

to be just as good as she'd promised. The sweetness of the caramel balanced nicely with the rich bite of the coffee. "Go on."

She sucked her bottom lip. "Basically, she asked me to deliver some bad news to my father, something about his past actions that may have come back to bite him in the rear end." She shook her head. "I don't want to say too much about the details."

He held up his hand. "That's fine. Feel free to tell me as much, or as little, as you like."

"Anyway, it was news to me, too. I don't even know if what I was asked to relay to him is true." She took a bite of her croissant and chewed.

"How did he react to this news?" While his curiosity grew by the second, he didn't feel it was his place to press her for more details about this mysterious bad news.

"He was angry, but he insisted it wasn't true." She sighed. "All I know is, just the knowledge that it's even a thing has changed the way I look at my father."

"Wow. It must be pretty serious."

"It is, and I wish my father could see it that way." She took another sip of coffee. "I tried to tell him that if he doesn't address this thing, true or not, it's not gonna just go away. He dismissed me." Her frustration came through in her tone.

What in the world is the big secret? Is the man sick? Did he commit a crime? There was no telling. So rather than press, he commiserated. "That sucks.

Sounds like your dad and mine are cut from the same stubborn cloth."

She gave a little chuckle. "Oh, really?"

"Absolutely. Last year my dad had pneumonia. Two days after he got back on his feet, he went on a dig in the South American rainforest. Just gallivanting around in all that dampness, as if he didn't just get out of the hospital." He shook his head. "Still can't believe my mom let him go."

Her brow inched up. "Dig? What exactly does he do for a living?"

"Oh, my parents—or 'the Doctors McCoy' as they're often called—are super nerdy. My dad, Stephen, is an archaeologist. My mom's name is Wanda, and she's an anthropologist."

Wide-eyed, she said, "Wow. Those sound like some pretty interesting jobs."

He shrugged. "I guess so, I'm just used to it since I grew up around it."

"Any siblings?" She posed the question with genuine interest.

His heart squeezed in his chest. "Um, yeah. I had a younger sister, Whitney. Unfortunately, we lost her in an…accident last year."

The sadness returned to her eyes. "Maxton, I'm so sorry. I hope I didn't upset you by being nosy."

He shook off the pain that coiled around his rib cage, threatening to strangle him like a snake. "Nah, it's cool. There was no way for you to know. It was an innocent question."

"I don't know if it'd help, but you could always borrow one of my siblings." A small grin showed on her face. "Take Miles. Hell, you'd be doing me a favor."

He laughed, amused by her offer. "No thanks. Ya brother a little too extra for me."

"That he is." She giggled.

He sat, watching her, in awe of the way the sound of her laughter warmed the places inside of him that were cold and soothed the ones that hurt.

Their conversation continued on, flowing as naturally as if they were two old friends who'd recently reunited. He didn't realize how long they'd been chatting until a barista alerted them that the coffee shop was closing.

"My bad. I hope I haven't kept you out too late," he said as he rose from his seat.

She shook her head. "I had a good time. I feel better now that I got some stuff off my chest." She paused, looking up at him through a fringe of dark lashes. "Thank you for listening."

"No problem." He tried to ignore the way his pulse quickened at her words. "I'd better go so I won't miss the next train."

"Where do you live?"

"Virginia Highlands," he answered.

She pulled her keys from her purse. "I'm in Druid Hills, so you're on the way. I'll drop you off."

They rode in companionable silence, and when they reached his complex, he started to get out. Pausing, he said, "Teagan, I hope this isn't too forward. But—"

"I'd really like to see you again." She lowered her eyes for a moment before meeting his gaze once more. "Do you want to hang out Saturday?"

Now it was his turn to be taken aback. "Yeah."

"Good." She smiled. "We'll work out the details tomorrow."

They said their good-nights, and with a wink, she drove away.

He stood on the curb for a long time, contemplating Sharrod's chastisement.

Yeah, I remember what I said about no romantic entanglements. But Teagan and I are just having fun, and there's no law against that. We're just hanging out, and that's all it is.

Seven

Saturday morning, Teagan answered the knock on her door with a smile. The smile fell when she was greeted by the retreating back of the delivery guy. Looking down, she saw the box containing the fancy litter and treats she ordered for her cat.

She hauled the heavy box inside, then closed the door with a sigh. Grabbing her keys from the hook on the wall, she used one to cut through the tape. Clicking her tongue, she called, "Here, Luna."

Moments later, her favorite hunk of black fur came hurtling in her direction. The cat tried to perch on top of the box…and promptly fell in with the contents.

Teagan laughed, tearing open the zipper pouch of treats and tossing some in the box with the cat.

"Here, girl. Have a snack." Leaving her cat to enjoy the goodies, she turned toward the full-length mirror mounted on her coat-closet door, checking her appearance once more. The blue-floral romper she'd chosen had a muted print and covered everything that needed coverage while still leaving enough skin exposed so she wouldn't spontaneously combust the moment she stepped into the Georgia heat.

Another knock sounded, and she went to answer it. Luna scrambled past her feet, retreating for the safety of the bedroom.

Guess that's why nobody has a "guard cat." When she opened the door this time and saw Maxton standing on her porch, she smiled. "Hey."

"Hey there." He grinned. "Did you remember to wear your bathing suit?"

She eased aside the corner of her romper's sleeve, showing off the black-and-white strap of her suit. "Yep."

He stared at her bared shoulder for a few long seconds, then blinked a few times. "And do you have a bag to bring it home in?"

She held up her duffle bag. "I've got all my essentials right here." She eyed him. "So, do I get to know where we're going now?"

He shook his head with a laugh. "Nope. It's a surprise."

Stepping out of the house, she locked the door and pulled it shut behind her. "Let's hope it's a good one. I can definitely see the appeal of getting in the water, with it being this hot." She wondered which pool or swimming hole he planned to take her to. Atlanta had plenty of them.

"That's the spirit." He held out his arm and escorted her off the porch to the driveway. "Nice house, by the way."

"Thanks. It's just enough space so I don't feel confined." They approached his car and she whistled. "Nice wheels, playboy." She gestured to the sleek black convertible parked behind her coupe. The car's top was let down, revealing the tan leather seats and lacquered wood-grain paneling inside.

He chuckled. "Thanks. I just rented it until the end of the month. I'll decide whether or not to extend my rental based on our progress with Swagg's album." With a flourish, he opened the passenger-side door. "You may enter the chariot, my lady."

Giggling, she let him help her into the buttery-soft seat, buckling herself in. Taking a pair of sunglasses from her purse, she slipped them on and prepared to enjoy the ride. Once he was in the driver's seat, she contented herself with watching the scenery fly by.

They left Druid Hills traveling west through Atkins Park, then going slightly south through Old Fourth Ward. Once they passed Central Park and headed into Sono, she said, "Are we going somewhere in Midtown or downtown?"

He nodded. "Very astute, Teagan."

Without any further clues, she returned to watching the familiar places they passed. As they slowly navigated through traffic on the northwest end of North Avenue, she realized Midtown was out. *Where could he be taking me in the downtown area that I need a bathing suit?* It could be anywhere from a poolside bar at one of the fancier hotels to the MLK Natatorium to the facility at Centennial Park.

Mercifully, her curiosity about their destination was soon alleviated, as he turned off of Luckie Street at the Georgia Aquarium. Still, that left her with a whole other set of questions. "When are you going to tell me what we're doing today?"

"I'm not. I'm just going to show you."

She blew out a breath. "Maxton."

"Just try to be patient. It'll be worth it, I promise." He pulled up to the entry of the parking deck, scanned a prepaid ticket and drove forward when the striped bar lifted to allow him inside.

Once they were parked, they headed inside the main building and she followed him to the second floor, to a reception desk marked Animal Interactions.

The moment she read the sign, something clicked in her brain. "Oh, snap, Maxton."

He glanced over his shoulder at her. "Hmm?"

She poked him in the back with her index finger. "We're going to interact with animals here? That sounds so cool!"

He laughed. "Yeah, when I heard you talking the other night at the coffee shop, I thought this sort of thing might be your jam." He handed his ID over to the woman behind the desk. "She'll need yours, too."

With excitement humming through her like a current, she fished her driver's license out of her back pocket and handed it over. He returned it to her shortly, and the aquarium employee then gestured for them to follow her.

She felt like a kid as she walked with them through the corridors of the aquarium, finally arriving at an area that felt decidedly behind the scenes. Joining a group of four others, she listened as a wet suit-clad aquarium diver briefed them on what they'd be doing.

"Welcome to the Shark and Ray Encounter at the Georgia Aquarium," she began. "Today, you'll get a chance to put on a suit just like the one I'm wearing and interact, up close and personal, with some of our sharks and rays." The woman continued on, talking about how they'd be given all the necessary equipment and allowed to change, but Teagan spent the rest of the speech half-listening, staring at Maxton.

He met her gaze. "You okay over there, shorty?"

"Rays? Really? They're my—"

"Favorite sea creature. I know, I remember you telling me that." He grinned, gave her shoulder a squeeze. "I called to see how many types of rays they have here—eleven, by the way—and the man on the phone said if rays were your thing, he had two spots left for this encounter."

Something inside Teagan bloomed, and at that

moment, she could barely compose herself against the swelling excitement. Another feeling rose, too. Gratitude. "Thank you, Maxton. This is the most thoughtful date I've ever been taken on."

He tilted his head to the side. "Fine as you are? Damn shame, but I'm glad I could be the one to do it for you."

For the next two hours, they learned about the various facets of shark and ray biology, their natural habitats and worldwide conservation efforts to keep their numbers up in the wild. During the second half, they changed into the provided wet suits so they could enter each animal's respective habitat in turn. The best part, however, came when Teagan got to stand between Maxton and an aquarium diver in chest-deep water, sprinkling plankton into the water. Two female rays circled around her, gliding through the water while devouring the treats, and as she watched them, she felt herself ascend to the halls of nerd Valhalla.

After the program ended, they returned to the locker rooms to dry off and get back into their street clothes. She got dressed quickly, wanting to warm up from the lingering chill, and waited in the hall for Maxton. Seeing his sneaker lying in the hallway, she went to pick it up. Dang, he must have dropped it.

She looked up to find him approaching her, wearing nothing but a pair of orange swim trunks. Beads of water clung to his muscled upper body and powerful thighs. Her eyes lingered at his waist for a moment, and the closer he got, the more she realized she was wet again, for entirely different reasons.

"Hey, you found my shoe." He reached for it. "I was looking all over for it."

She handed it over.

"Thanks. I'll be out in a sec." He turned and re-entered the men's locker room, showing off a back view that was just as delightful as the front.

She flopped down on the single bench in the hall, doing her best to recover before he came back. As it turned out, Maxton had quite a body beneath his stylish wardrobe. And even though she knew it was too soon to be thinking that way, parts of her wanted to see more of…what he had to offer.

He emerged again, fully dressed. "Ready to go?"

She nodded and stood. "This was amazing. Thank you again."

He stuck out his arm. "You're welcome. The date's not over, though. I'm taking you to lunch." As they started to walk down the corridor toward the reception desk where they'd checked in, he said, "You know, you liked this so much, it's gonna be pretty hard to top it on a second date. That is…if you wanna do this again."

She smiled up at him. "Oh, I'm sure you'll come up with something, playboy."

Seated at a secluded table inside Hudson Grille on Marietta, Maxton looked across the table at his companion. Her attention was on the menu lying on the table in front of her; his attention was on her face. She was so beautiful, and the lingering joy in her expression made her even more so.

She looked up as if she felt his gaze on her. "What is it, Maxton?"

He shook his head, focusing on his own menu. "Nothing."

He had a few minutes to study the menu before the waiter returned with their drinks. "Here's your Sweetwater IPA, sir, and your iced tea and water, ma'am." Sitting the glasses down, he pulled out his pen and pad. "You folks ready to order?"

Maxton looked at Teagan.

"Sure. I'll have the jerk-spiced salmon sandwich with the regular fries on the side, please."

The waiter jotted that down. "Good choice. And you, sir?"

"Let me get the Four Horsemen burger with a side of sweet potato fries."

"Gotcha. I'll get that right out to you." Taking their menus, the waiter disappeared.

She leaned forward, resting her forearms on the table. "I had so much fun at the aquarium today. I never even knew I had an interest in sharks, but I learned so many neat little facts about them."

He smiled. "I see you're going to keep talking about this forever, and I love it." She radiated delight, and it warmed his heart to see her so happy, so far removed from the moment he'd approached her car and found her sobbing.

"Probably." She laughed. "I couldn't help noticing how comfortable you seemed in the water. Are you an avid diver or something?"

He shrugged. "I wouldn't classify myself as avid, but I've been on three or four scuba dives since I was about ten. You should really take lessons, considering how much you enjoyed today. I mean, that was just in a tank. Imagine how geeked you'd be in the open ocean."

She tilted her head slightly to the right as if thinking it over. "I'll have to take that into consideration."

"This wasn't my first time swimming with rays. Or sharks, for that matter. This was just the first time I did it in a controlled environment."

She leaned forward, her brown eyes sparkling, "Well, tell me all about your last ray encounter, Jacques Cousteau."

Laughing, he launched into the story. "Word. So this was about three years back. Mom, Dad, Whitney and I were in Jamaica on a family trip. We were snorkeling at this place called Doctor's Cave Beach, right by Montego Bay. We're all swimming in a line, basically, to make sure we stay together. Anyway, we swam through a cave and came out on the other side. There were these two young rays, circling and playing in the water. We kept our distance but followed them for as long as we could. My dad took, like, a million pictures with his underwater camera. Finally, they sped up and zoomed off, leaving us behind." He paused, realizing what this moment represented. "You know, this is the first time I've shared a memory of my sister with someone, without getting upset, in a really long time."

Her expression softened, but her smile remained as she reached across the table and grasped his hand. "I'm honored."

Their food came, and as Maxton sank his teeth into the juicy, flavorful burger, he immediately felt the burn. It was one of the spiciest on the menu, featuring jalapeño, red pepper, habanero and a house-made special sauce called Scorpion Stinger—who knew what kind of spices were in that. Even as a lover of spicy food, he had to admit that this packed the heat. Swallowing, he said, "Yikes. I can see how this burger got its name."

Smiling, Teagan asked, "Too spicy?"

He shook his head, raising the burger for another bite. "Nah. I can hang."

"You sure?" She looked skeptical. "Because you're sweating."

He chewed and swallowed another mouthful of beef, tomato and spiciness. A trickle of sweat slid down his face, and he grabbed a napkin from the pile in the center of the table. Mopping his brow, he grinned. "That's how I like it. Keeps the sinuses clear and the mind sharp."

"If you say so." She folded a crisp fry into her mouth and washed it down with tea.

By the time he finished his food, he'd built quite a pile of napkins to keep the sweat out of his eyes.

"Whew. The fries helped, but not as much as I wanted them to." He signaled the waiter for a glass of water and drank it in one long swig.

Pushing aside her own plate, Teagan remarked, "The jerk salmon was really flavorful and delicious. And not too spicy," she added with a wink.

He chuckled. "Whatever. I finished the burger, didn't I?" He knew he'd probably pay the price in heartburn later, but she didn't need to know that.

After he paid the check and left a nice tip for their server, he stood next to the table and extended his arm. "Ready?"

She smiled up at him as she stood and looped her arm through his. "You're such a gentleman."

"Just one of my many sides," he said as they walked out of the restaurant.

He drove her home, pulling into her driveway just after two. There he opened the passenger-side door, helped her to her feet and escorted her onto the porch. The house, a decent-size ranch with charcoal-gray siding, blue shutters and a decorative stone walkway, looked like the perfect little starter home for a small family. "This seems like a big house for one person. Do you have a roommate or something?"

She shook her head as she pulled her keys out of her purse. "Nope, it's just me and Luna, my cat. The house has two bedrooms and two baths, and that's perfect for us."

"Gotcha."

The lock clicked and she pushed the door open. "If you've got time to come in, I'll show you around."

He followed her inside. For the next few minutes, she showed him her home. The interior was much more modern than the exterior, indicating a recent remodel. "The house was built in the eighties. I bought it two years ago. I upgraded the flooring, the cabinets and the countertops myself, with a little help from my dad and my brothers." She gestured around. "I'm really proud of the way it turned out."

"I can see why." The sealed, ash-gray wood flooring complimented the soft yellow paint on the walls. The open layout allowed him to see straight through the family room and dining room into the kitchen, which had soft gray cabinetry, granite countertops and stainless-steel appliances.

She took him through an arched opening on the left side of the dining room, into a hallway, as a black streak raced by their feet. "That would be Luna. She's shy. There's a bathroom here," she gestured to the only open door. "The other one is in the primary suite." Cracking open a door, she let him look inside. "This is my home-office-slash-craft room."

He looked inside, noting the neat, meticulous setup. One side of the room had her narrow, whitewashed desk with her laptop, a printer and chair, and the opposite wall hosted a similar desk, the top of which was covered with various bins and cups holding art supplies. The wall directly across from the door had a picture window with a bench seat in a small niche, the walls of which held mounted shelves holding various books and knickknacks. "Nice."

She took him back to the front door.

He eyed her and asked, "Isn't there something I didn't get to see?"

She smiled. "If you mean my bedroom, you gotta earn it, playboy."

"Sounds like a challenge," he quipped.

She shook her head. "No. More of a requirement."

He laughed, then gently dragged the tip of his index finger along her jawline. "You're going to make me work for this. I just know it."

Her only answer was a sultry smile. "We'll just have to see what happens."

"Truth is, I really don't have the time for a relationship right now."

If she took offense at his statement, she didn't show it. "Neither do I."

"So, what are we doing here?"

She shrugged. "A fling? A dalliance? I don't think it really matters what we call it, so long as we both understand what it is…and what it isn't."

Their gazes met and held, and the sparkle of mischief in her eyes threatened to do him in. "Enlighten me, Teagan. What will we be doing, exactly?"

"We hang out…have a little fun. No strings, no commitments. And above all, we don't let this thing interfere with our work or our lives." She pressed her open palm against his chest. "That is, if you think you can handle it."

"Secms reasonable." *I like this approach. Seems like we're on one accord.*

Her smile deepened. "Tomorrow is my only other free day for a while. Why don't you meet me at the Creamery, right near Piedmont Park? Say, around 7?"

"I'll be there." He wanted to kiss her but couldn't read her thoughts on the matter. So he grazed his fingertip over her soft, glossy lips instead.

"See you then," she whispered.

Satisfied, he opened the front door and stepped out into the afternoon sunshine.

Eight

Teagan stood near the main entrance to Piedmont Park on Sunday evening, placing herself out of the flow of traffic. The day was slightly overcast, mercifully lowering the temperature into the upper seventies. After a day spent in her office/craft room, working on an abstract watercolor she'd been tweaking for a few weeks, it was nice to get some fresh air.

She'd chosen a simple but stylish white maxi dress, printed with black roses. The thin straps left her arms bared, and the bejeweled white sandals on her feet had a thick, contoured sole that made them comfortable for walking.

She let her eyes scan the clusters of people passing through the entrance until, finally, she spotted Maxton across the street. Holding her hand up high, she gestured to him. She watched as he waited at the crossing signal, and when it was safe, he jogged over to her.

"Hey there. Have you been waiting long?"

"No." She shook her head. "I've only been here a few minutes."

"Good. Wouldn't want to keep you waiting."

She let her gaze over him. He wore black twill slacks with a silver chain dangling between two of the loops on his right hip. He'd paired the slacks with dark sneakers and a black T-shirt with an interesting design. "Is that Jimi Hendrix on your shirt?"

"Yeah. If you look closely, you'll see that his portrait is made up of…"

She leaned closer. "The lyrics to the song 'Purple Haze.'"

"Good eye." He winked. "Now, let's get some ice cream, shall we?"

She linked arms with him and they walked the short distance to the Creamery. The brightly painted food truck often set up in the park during the summer months and usually drew quite a crowd with its homemade ice cream. "Oh, good. There's only, like, four people ahead of us."

"They've got a lot of good flavors," Maxton remarked, scanning the menu painted on the side of the truck.

When it was their turn, she stepped up to the window. "A double scoop of fudge ripple on a waffle cone, please."

"I'll take a double scoop of pistachio in a waffle bowl." Maxton pulled out a few bills from his wallet. "We're together."

The worker cashed them out, and they moved to the left window to allow the next person to order while they waited. A few minutes later, a second worker handed them their order with a smile. "Enjoy!"

Taking their treats to a bench parked beneath a shady willow, they sat down. Neither of them spoke as they dug in. The breeze rustled through the tree's branches as she enjoyed the cool, creamy flavors of vanilla and chocolate dancing across her tongue. Before she knew it, she'd devoured the first scoop.

She glanced to her side and saw Maxton staring at her. He was still eating, but his gaze was locked on her face so intently, it was a miracle he could still guide his spoon to his mouth. At that moment, it occurred to her how she must look to him, dragging her tongue over the heap of fudge ripple. She paused. "Sorry. I must look like a moose licking ice off a windowpane."

He chuckled. "That's a very creative metaphor."

"I saw it on a television special about Alaska once, and I've never been able to get that image out of my head."

"I definitely wouldn't make that comparison." He passed his tongue over his lower lip. "I think it's kinda sexy."

She swallowed, not sure how to respond to the tingle of arousal that went down her back.

"So," Maxton said, spooning up some of his ice cream, "tell me about your family."

She drew a deep breath. "Describing my family members can be a little hard, so I'll try to be succinct. There are seven of us. My mom, Addison, is a martial arts and vegan food enthusiast. My dad, Caleb, is an old-fashioned gent who still owns seersucker and occasionally smokes cigars. They founded 404 before any of us were born."

"I see. And your siblings?"

He appeared genuinely interested, so she continued. "There are five of us. The oldest is Nia. She's uptight. Major oldest-sibling syndrome. Next is Blaine. He's the rebel. Then, there's Gage. He's overly serious, although his recent marriage seems to have made him a little less anal. Then, there's Miles and me. He's the older twin because he used my head as a launchpad so he could be born first. He's a fitness buff and something of a player."

Maxton laughed, hard. Setting his ice cream down on his lap, he said, "What?"

"Stop laughing. I'm serious. He just bogarted his way out, it's something he still does to this day." She shook her head. "You met him."

He recovered from his laughing fit, grabbing his waffle bowl again. "That I did, and he does seem like…a handful."

She sighed. "He is. But I still love him. I love my

whole family, even though they get on my nerves sometimes."

"You gave me some…rather colorful descriptions there." He snapped off a piece of his bowl. "But now I'm curious to know how you describe yourself."

She sucked on her lower lip. "I don't know. That's kind of a tall order on such short notice. I exist in multitudes, you know."

"I sensed that." He gave another low, rumbling chuckle. "How about this. Describe yourself with three adjectives."

"Hmm. Let me think about it while I finish this." She ate the remainder of her rapidly melting ice cream, turning slightly away from him. Then she crunched on the top half of the waffle cone. Folding up the rest in a napkin, she tossed it in the metal wastebasket positioned nearby. Tapping her chin, she said, "I'm gonna go with *focused*, *practical* and *intelligent*."

He nodded. "Okay, I see. From what I know of you, I can agree with all of those. But I think you're definitely leaving some things out."

She punched him playfully in the shoulder. "That's your fault. You only gave me three adjectives."

"You're right, you're right. My bad." He rubbed his upper arm. "Ease up on me, slugger. I'm gonna add some descriptors if I may."

"I'll allow it." She noticed a light green streak

near the right corner of his mouth. "Hold on." Reaching for a napkin, she swiped the stain away.

He gave her a soft smile, one that made the skin around his eye crinkle. "Thanks. Anyway, I'd say you're beautiful, witty, thoughtful and—" he paused, letting his gaze move slowly over her form "—shapely."

Warmth bloomed in her chest, and she knew it wasn't a result of the Georgia heat but rather the hungry gaze of the handsome man sitting next to her. "You're laying it on thick today, I see."

He shrugged. "Maybe, but I'm honest."

"I suppose. I'm everything you described me to be, and more." She giggled. "Wanna hit the trail before it gets dark? Walk off some of these calories?"

"Sure."

They walked to the trailhead of the shortest trail and entered it. The sun was sinking low on the horizon, though it was mostly shrouded by clouds. She looked up, seeing the oranges and pinks of sunset had begun to paint the sky, visible through the canopy of leaves above.

He reached for her hand and held it within his. "This cool with you?"

She nodded.

"Just checking. I know we're still working out the details of our little liaison." He winked.

She looked his way, taking in his profile, the strong jaw, the thick brows and the full lips. "I like your approach. Since you're a light touch, I might be giving you a little more leeway than you imagined."

He stopped walking, looked at her. "Oh, really."

"Really." She wriggled her hand free from his, then traced her fingertips up both his arms. Hooking her hands behind his neck, she asked, "Can I have three words to describe you now?"

He nodded, never taking his eyes off her.

"I'm gonna say *handsome*, *talented* and *irresistible*."

He opened his mouth to respond, but she covered it with hers before he could. His strong arms wrapped around her waist, pulling her body against his. She relished the feel of his firm, muscled torso pressed against her.

The kiss deepened, and she was so swept up in it that it took her a few beats to notice the first round of drops of water hitting her skin.

She drew back from him, touched his cheek. "I think it's raining."

"It is. We'd better go."

As they dashed back up the trail toward the entrance, the rain grew heavier, fat drops pelting them at every step. Running over the wet grass, they passed a few other folks in the same situation, picking up their pace or ducking beneath trees or other structures to find shelter from the weather.

"Where did you park?" he called to her over the rain.

"In the deck on Monroe!"

By the time he left her at her car, she was soaked to the bone, and shivering. But she knew the sensation rocketing through her body had nothing to do with being cold and everything to do with the irresistible man she'd just dashed through the park with. Something was happening between them… something special.

Monday evening, Maxton shut and locked his front door behind him, sighing into his empty apartment. He leaned his back against the cool metal door for a few moments, trying to gather his rollicking emotions.

He couldn't recall ever experiencing a day that seemed so long. Since the moment he'd dragged himself out of bed this morning, he'd been fighting to stay focused, to remain upbeat. Now, alone in his home, he felt the weight of keeping up the appearance finally lift from his shoulders.

Unfortunately, the sadness remained.

Today, Whitney would have been twenty-seven.

He pushed himself off the door and trudged to the living room, setting his bass on the armchair before taking a seat on the sofa. He pulled off the black sneakers he'd worn into the studio, then buried his sock-clad feet in the thick pile of his throw rug as he slumped against the backrest.

The ball of tears stuck in his throat threatened to rise at any moment, and after keeping them in all day, he was too tired to care anymore. His eyes welled, and he sprawled there, letting the tears slide down. It wasn't like the last time he'd cried, all those weeks ago. He didn't sob, didn't wail. Just silently mourned his little sister, his gaze on the ceiling, his vision swimming.

His phone rang then, the steady vibration against his thigh drawing him back to reality. Brushing away the lingering wetness on his face, he took his phone out of his pocket and answered the incoming video call. "Hey, Ma. How are you?"

Wanda McCoy's face came into view, or at least the lower half of it. "Hey, Maxie. I'm alright, you doing okay?"

"Yeah, Ma." He cringed. "Ma, you're too close to the camera again."

"I can see you. Matter of fact, when's the last time you shaved, boy?"

He shook his head. "I'm growing out my beard. Fix your camera, Ma. All I can see is your mouth."

"Oh, for goodness' sake." The picture on the screen became shaky and shifted around, going from her mouth and chin to the ceiling, to the floral wallpaper in the kitchen before finally settling on her full face and upper torso. She was sitting at the kitchen table, inside their family home in the suburbs of Calabasas. A black-velvet headband held her salt-and-pepper curls back from her aged brown face, and her dark eyes squinted as she looked into the camera. "How's that, son? Can you see me now?"

"Yes, Ma, that's better." He smiled. "Sorry I

couldn't make it home, but I'm just getting into the thick of this gig with Lil Swagg."

"Lil who?" Her brows eased together, a show of genuine confusion.

"Lil Swagg, Ma. He's a young rapper out of the Bronx. And even though you're not into that kind of music, at least the kid's got a good ear. Not many artists his age would go to the trouble and expense of recording with a live band over a drum machine and some manufactured beats."

She pursed her lips. "Hmm. That does set him apart from the rest, I suppose." She reached off-screen, then raised a glass of dark-colored liquid to her lips.

"Ma, are you drinking soda pop?"

She frowned. "Oh, hush. It's that sugar-free cola, so don't you fuss."

"Alright, I won't. So, how's Dad?"

"He's still with Dr. Sutton in Sicily. They're working in the Valley of the Temples."

He scratched his chin, thinking back. "Oh, yeah, I remember him talking about that. He's been trying to get in on that action for a while now, hasn't he?"

She nodded. "Yes, child. Talked about it nonstop for weeks. I'm just glad the department chose him to go this time so I can stop hearing about it."

"Ma, you know he'll come home with a million stories and probably a few souvenirs."

"I know. But I enjoy that part." Her lips tilted up into a small smile. "He always brings me back something I can use, whether it's an artifact or an anecdote."

She quieted, her smile fading.

For a few moments, they simply looked at each other. In the silence, an understanding passed between them, one of shared grief.

Finally, she spoke. "I…went by Whitney's grave this morning."

He nodded. "The headstone in place, right?"

"It's there. I had no idea having a custom one made with her image engraved on it would take so long." She sighed. "Anyway, it's there now, and it looks so nice. I'll text you a picture of it later."

"Okay."

Her eyes grew damp. "I took her some flowers. I had the florist make me up an arrangement of orange mums with a birthday ribbon around the pot."

"Her favorite color. I'm sure she would love it, Ma." He paused. "Thanks…for going over there."

"Of course."

She quieted again, and the corners of her mouth drooped. Her eyes began to dampen, and she sniffled. But she quickly plastered on a smile as she got up, taking the phone with her on a walk through the house.

He watched the screen as she entered his sister's childhood room. The space remained untouched, down to the bed being unmade from the last time she'd slept in it before the accident. "I keep saying I'm going to clean this room out, donate some of her things. Lord knows there are folks out there who could use them."

"There's no rush, Ma." He wanted her to know she didn't have to bear the burden alone, as she was apt to do as the family matriarch. "When I finish this gig, I can come home. You know, help you go through it and make some decisions."

"Closet full of clothes in here," she said, turning the camera toward the open closet door. "Stuff she couldn't wear anymore. Old baby clothes, even."

"Keep the baby clothes, Ma."

"I probably will. Myrtle was saying something about getting them put in a shadowbox or something like that."

He nodded at the mention of her good friend and colleague, Dr. Myrtle Reeves. Myrtle taught in the English department at Cal Lutheran in Woodland Hills, where his mother taught in the global studies department. "Sounds like a good way to preserve them."

The image panned around the room, showing the familiar lavender walls. Taped to them were many of her school awards, her dreamcatcher that she'd made one summer at camp and a good eight or nine posters, all of the same artist. "Wow. I'd almost forgotten how obsessed Whit was with Tupac."

She sighed, still off camera. "Yes, yes. She loved him, even though I thought his lyrics were a little too brash. I never made a fuss because your father and

I tried to let you kids enjoy things, let you explore and develop your own personalities."

That was true; he couldn't ever remember his parents forcing them to do anything. They'd discuss; they'd explain; they'd even ask firmly. But they never pushed. And in response, he and his sister had, with few exceptions, remained on the straight and narrow. "You're right, his lyrics could be a little rough at times. But Pac was a wunderkind, a true poet. Did you know there are entire college courses devoted to his lyrics now?"

She turned the camera back to her face, showing her wide eyes. "No, I didn't. Obviously, we don't have those classes at Cal Lutheran."

"Yeah. But they're a thing. I think after he was gone, people started to look back and see his genius." He thought back on the late-night conversations he'd had with his sister about Tupac's songs. "But Whit knew back then. She had good taste."

The tears filled her eyes then, and her breathing grew heavy. "I miss my baby girl, Maxie. I miss her so, so much."

He felt his own eyes watering again. "I know, Ma. I miss her, too."

She sat down on the end of the twin bed and sobbed.

There was nothing he could do, no comfort he could offer. They were both caught in this storm of pain and grief, this dark chasm that he feared had no light at the other end. He wished he could reach through the phone and pull her into his arms. But that was impossible. So instead, he simply let her cry, watching over her as she emptied out some of the hurt. He felt that familiar squeezing in his chest, and he set his phone down and drew several long, deep breaths.

She wiped her face, getting up from the bed. As she left Whitney's room, closing the door behind her, she said, "Sorry about that, son."

"Don't apologize, Ma. Do you remember what Pastor Yates said about grief?"

She nodded. "It's love with nowhere to go."

"Right." He dried his face with the tail of his shirt. "It's hard now, and it might be hard for a long time. But we're going to get through this."

"I know we will. Sometimes, I just can't see that." She ran her hand over her hair. "Let me go on and get this laundry done. Have you eaten?"

"No, not yet."

"Well, eat something, baby. And try to involve some vegetables."

He chuckled. Same old Ma. "I will, Ma. I love you."

"I love you, too, baby." She offered him a watery smile before disconnecting the call.

Taking a deep breath, he got up from the sofa and went to see what he had in the fridge. Removing a bagged salad from the crisper, he poured some on a plate. Teagan's face popped into his mind.

He recalled their lunch on Saturday and the way

he'd just naturally told her a story about his family, about Whitney. She'd listened and, in doing so, had given him a gift: a chance to relive the moment and feel the love he had for his sister, without the pain and guilt of losing her.

As he poured the dressing over the salad, he smiled.

Teagan Woodson was nothing less than incredible, and he knew this would be an unforgettable fling.

Nine

Teagan stood by the sofa inside the outer suite of Studio One, listening as Lil Swagg and Rick compared notes on the project at hand.

"I think we're making good progress," Rick said. "We've got the first two tracks in the bag, and we'll get the third and maybe the fourth done today."

Swagg nodded, his eyes still locked on the screen of his phone. He wore a black tracksuit with purple piping, and the words Bronx Swagg emblazoned across his chest. The words were partially hidden by yet another heavy, jewel-encrusted chain, this one featuring a large pendant in the shape of a microphone. "You right, Rick. We're looking good right now. We just need to keep up that momentum."

Wondering how he could even see the screen

through the lenses of his dark sunglasses, Teagan nodded her agreement. "I think we're right where we need to be. I'm cleaning up the files as we go, so the finished song files should be super clean and easy for Chanel to put her finishing touch on."

"I'm sure she'll love that." Swagg glanced up, smiled. "And if that's the case, I can definitely recommend 404 to some of my homies back home that's looking for that upscale recording experience."

Teagan grinned. "Thanks. We'd be honored to get that endorsement."

"No problem, Miss Teagan." He raised his fist and bumped it with hers. "You got real skills at the board, and I respect your professionalism. Real talk."

"I'm happy to help. I'm a total nerd for sound engineering. That's why I work in here instead of in the c-suite upstairs." She felt the bounce in her step as she made her way back to the workstation and sat down. The on-screen clock displayed the time: 9:32. The musicians would be there within the half hour to get the day's session underway. Deciding to use this bit of downtime wisely, she opened the file for track one of Swagg's albums and ran it through the system's automatic optimization program. The program displayed an on-screen graph, showing its progress, and she watched it for a few beats before taking out her phone.

A text message from Miles appeared on the screen.

Hike this week?

Swiping the message away, she shook her head. *I barely made it on the last walk, and now he's asking me to hike with him? Sheesh.*

Rick's voice cut into her thoughts. "We've got a guest coming today, to lay down a verse."

She turned her chair to face him. "Did you talk to the guys at the security desk about that?"

"Yeah, I did."

"As long as Tate and Owen know, we should be good." She turned back toward the workstation, anticipating how crowded it would be with more people in the room. It wasn't ideal, but she tried to respect the wishes of her artists so as not to interfere with the creative process. *That reminds me, it's about time I lobby Nia and my parents about moving to a newer, bigger building so I can have more space in my studio.* Whenever the next true hip-hop supergroup came along, she wanted to be ready. Keeping her eyes on the screen, she kept her ears open.

Swagg said, "Rick, who the hell is coming here today? I didn't request anybody for a guest spot. I thought we were gonna record that stuff later when we got back with Chanel in NYC."

"Don't worry, man. It's all arranged. Trust me, this collab is gon' set the hip-hop world on fire."

"I hope so." Swagg sounded less than convinced. Mike walked in then, carrying his keyboard case. The other three musicians followed behind him in a lopsided line, with Maxton bringing up the rear.

Teagan exchanged greetings with each of them as they passed. As usual, Maxton lingered.

Today, he wore a pair of black jeans that sat just at the top of his hips, showing off the gray waistband of a pair of designer boxer briefs. His black tee had a grayscale image of The Notorious B.I.G.'s face on it, along with the quote It's All Good, Baby, Baby. His shiny dark curls were swept to one side, and she could see something silver dangling from his left ear. "Hey, Teagan."

"Hey, yourself." She pointed. "New piercing?"

He grinned. "Yeah, got it last night. It's a letter W."

She nodded, understanding the meaning. "I like it. Looks good."

She heard Swagg whistle, then say, "I see my bass player got the juice with the ladies, too! I see you, homie!"

Maxton laughed. "Let me get my ass in the booth."

She stifled a giggle. "Yeah, you do that."

He went inside and shut the door behind him. She watched through the glass partition as the musicians set up to start the session. When everyone was in place, she engaged the suite's intercom-enabled sound system. "Y'all ready?"

A chorus of affirmative answers came over the speakers.

"Good deal. I'm gonna start playback on track three." She tapped the appropriate icons on the touchscreen of her workstation. The band picked up on it immediately, which didn't really surprise her considering the amount of time they'd spent working on it already. *They probably have the melody memorized by now.*

Swagg got up and stood near the counter, bobbing his head in time with the music. "Man, they're sounding good today. I like this."

"I agree. Maybe they practiced in their spare time," she joked, knowing full well Maxton had spent the better part of his weekend with her. That, however, was privileged information.

It took about ninety minutes before the instrumental track was completed to Swagg's satisfaction. He clapped his hands together. "That's it. That's the one right there."

"Great." Teagan saved the audio file.

Rick appeared beside them. "Right on time, too. Vic Grip and his people should be here any minute."

"Vic Grip? Hell, yeah!" Swagg nodded.

A knock sounded at the door. Rick opened it.

Teagan looked toward the three men who entered, all of them dressed similarly in baggy jeans and oversize tees, heavy chains around their necks. The one in the front declared, "What's up? Vic Grip and Money J are in the building."

Swagg frowned, turning to Rick. "What the fuck, Rick? Money J? I hate that crazy motherfucker."

Rick held up his hands. "I didn't know Money J was coming, I swear. I only invited Vic. He said he'd be bringing a couple folks with him."

Swagg's eyes flashed. "And you didn't ask him for names or nothing?"

"My bad, Swagg. I didn't even know they hang together." Rick's eyes darted back and forth between his artist and his guests.

Rick moved quickly to stand between Swagg and his guests, and the gaggle of bodies effectively blocked Teagan from scooting her chair away from the workstation.

Teagan, aware of the rising tension, turned her chair as much as she could. "Gentlemen, do we have a problem here?" She poised her hand over the handset of the desk phone next to her station.

"Nah, shawty," one of the visitors said, stalking closer to Swagg. He was the smaller one of the group but still wide enough to take up space. He wore a backward cap and had two teardrops tattooed beneath his right eye. "Ain't no problem, if Swagg keep my name out his mouth."

"It's not my fault your bars are garbage, J." Swagg folded his arms over his chest.

A vein popped in the man's neck. "See, that's that shady shit I'm talking about."

"It ain't shade. I'm just spittin' facts." Swagg's lips curled into a disdainful smile.

Money J pounded his fist into his hand. "Okay. I see I'm gonna have to knock that smirk off your face."

Teagan stood then. "Oh, no. Take that mess outside before you damage my equipment." She pointed at the door, and in doing so, touched one of the men's chest.

He sneered at her. "Don't touch me." He raised his hand.

The door to the booth swung open and Maxton strafed through a narrow gap in the tangle of bodies.

A second later, a flying fist hit Maxton square in his right eye, and he cursed.

All hell broke loose then as the men began swinging their fists and shouting obscenities. Teagan felt the backs of her knees being pushed into her chair as the men rumbled their way past her. Rick backed up toward the sofa only to have Swagg pushed into him. The entire time, Maxton kept his body wrapped around Teagan as the chaos and noise swirled around them.

Mike and Sharrod came from the booth and entered the fray, trying to pull Money J and Vic off Swagg and Rick. Brady hung back, his eyes darting toward the door.

The brute who'd tried to hit her remained there, effectively blocking the way out. He wore a crooked grin on his face, and she could tell he was enjoying the carnage he'd visited upon her domain. *What a grade A, first-class asshole.*

Enough of this. Teagan stretched past Maxton's hold, reached back and grabbed the handset, using the bottom of it to bang the number two key. Holding up the receiver, she shouted, "Security! Studio One!"

* * *

Maxton ignored the throbbing in his head, watching through his watery, partially closed eye as two burly, uniformed security officers elbowed their way into the room, with one guard slapping a zip tie around the wrists of the man who'd been trapping them all in the suite. Brady helped the guard drag him away while Sharrod and Mike helped the other guard subdue Vic and Money J.

He could feel the slight tremor in her body as he held her and hear the rapid breaths she took. She was afraid but refused to let it show on her stony face. She was a trooper, and he respected that. But the fact remained that she shouldn't have been subjected to such base behavior, especially not in her place of work.

It was the peak of immaturity. They were grown men, carrying on a pissing contest in the middle of the workday, like a bunch of bored youngsters. *This is precisely why I don't do that macho bravado bullshit. It's all fun and games until somebody gets hurt.* And as irked as he was by the shiner he'd gotten, he knew he'd have been even more pissed if Teagan was the one nursing the bruise.

As the so-called guests were dragged out, cursing, Maxton finally released his hold on Teagan. She flopped onto her chair, dropping her head in her hands.

"What the hell was that?" Maxton couldn't remember the last time he'd been so pissed. "I think you two owe Teagan an apology for this bullshit."

Rick, righting his clothing, shook his head. "Apparently, it was very bad judgment on my part. I apologize, Teagan."

It was quiet for a moment, so Maxton eyed Swagg.

Swagg, wiping a bit of blood from his lower lip, offered a solemn nod. "I'm sorry about this. I'm so freakin' embarrassed."

"Y'all brought way too much excitement into my studio." Her voice was shaky but determined. "See that you don't do it again. And I hope you know whatever damage was done will be billed to you and your artist." Teagan fought hard to keep the anger out of her voice. "I'm going to suspend recording for now, pending a final decision from the CEO."

"Got it," Rick said as he and Swagg departed.

Left alone with Teagan, Maxton let out a pent-up breath. "Are you alright?"

"I'm fine, thanks to you." She stroked her fingertips along his jawline.

Her touch soothed the ache in his head. "I wasn't about to let that jackass hit you."

"Chivalry is alive and well, I see." She gifted him with a soft kiss on the cheek. "I'm more concerned about you. That eye is about four shades of purple." She stood up. "Let me get you some ice, and then I'm taking you to urgent care."

He shook his head. "I don't want you to trouble yourself. Sharrod can take me."

"Did you take a fist to the eye for Sharrod?" She looked at him pointedly.

"No."

"Then, hush, and let me do this for you." She spun and marched out of the room.

After she left, he eased himself onto her seat. *What a day.*

Sharrod entered a moment later. "Damn, Max. You look a hot mess. You alright, bro?"

"Obviously, I got a black eye outta this deal." He resisted the urge to touch his eye. He could feel the tightness in the surrounding skin and had only a sliver of vision left on that side. "You think it's gonna heal well?"

Sharrod grimaced. "I don't know. It's pretty gnarly." He gave him a gentle slap on the shoulder. "Good looking out for Miss Teagan, though. Come on, I'll swing you by the ER."

"She's gonna take me to urgent care."

"You sure? It's no problem." His friend appeared genuinely concerned.

"She insisted. Trust me, you don't want the smoke with her." He chuckled, shaking his head. "This whole mess got her low-key pissed."

Sharrod threw up his hands. "Alright. Well, let me make myself scarce. Call me when you make it home, okay?"

"I will," Maxton promised. After his friend left, he had a few moments alone to process what had happened. He'd been in the center of an actual, real-life rap beef. And as cool as it sometimes seemed on social media, he found the consequences of such an encounter to be far more inconvenient than entertaining.

She reentered the room then with a stack of napkins and a plastic bag filled with crushed ice. She stooped, bringing a napkin to his face, and dabbing gently. "Just cleaning up the blood a little bit."

He nodded, his eyes locked on the swell of her cleavage that was visible above the square neckline of her short-sleeved top. The garment's golden hue accentuated the glow in her skin.

"Here, hold this against your eye." She stood, handing him the baggie of ice.

He dutifully pressed it to his swollen eye, wincing at the blistering cold.

"Okay. I'll grab your bass and walk you to my car."

"Alright," he said, standing. "Are you sure my case will fit in your car?" He tried to imagine how the bulky shell would fit in her little two-door coupe.

"We'll make it work unless want to leave it in the booth." She shrugged. "The doors will be locked."

He shook his head. "Nah. We don't really know when we'll be back in session yet, right?"

"That's true. Wait here. I'll go grab it."

He watched while she entered the booth, slipped the bass into the hard-shell case and snapped it shut. As she maneuvered it around the space, she said, "This isn't even as heavy as I thought it would be."

She grabbed her purse from the counter and slung the strap over her shoulder. "Come on, let's go."

He followed her outside, still holding the ice pack to his eye. In the parking lot, he saw the police talking to the security guards while Money J and his crew cooled their heels in the backs of two separate squad cars.

It took some work, but they managed to get his instrument into the back seat. After that, they climbed inside and she drove him away from the studio.

They entered the semi-empty interior of Quick Med Urgent Care and walked over to the check-in desk.

"Can I help you folks—?" The scrubs-clad employee behind the desk stopped midsentence as she looked up from the paperwork in front of her. "Ouch."

Maxton chuckled. "Yeah. It's been a bit of a day."

"How long is the wait for someone to patch him up?" Teagan asked.

The nurse typed into the computer in front of her. "It's not too bad. About twenty or thirty minutes."

"That's fine." Maxton stayed at the desk long enough to fill out the paperwork on the tablet she handed him, then he and Teagan took a seat in the far corner of the waiting room. There were only four other people there: an elderly couple and a woman with a small child on her lap.

"You know, I think you're pretty brave for stepping in the way you did. I respect that."

He shrugged. "As I said, I could tell he was going to swing and I wasn't having it. I was brought up better than that. I'd never raise my hand to a woman."

"Being around my brothers all the time, I think I take for granted that men will do what's right when it comes to how they treat women. Today, I got a pretty unpleasant reminder that's not always the case." She offered a crooked smile. "I appreciate what you did, Maxton."

"Guys are quick to say, 'not all men,' but I believe in putting my principles in action rather than standing by and watching other men misbehave." He stared at her with the only good eye he had at the moment and felt his heart do a somersault. "Thank you. For bringing me here and for being so kind."

She smiled. "A girl's gotta treat her knight in shining armor special, you know."

"McCoy?" someone called. "Maxton?"

The moment fizzled as he turned toward the sound, raising his hand instinctively. "I'll be back."

"I'll be waiting."

He followed the nurse and, over the next half hour, sat while his eye was cleaned, treated with ointment and patched up. When he emerged, Teagan stood. "Very fashionable," she said, gesturing to the small bandage beside his eye.

"You know it. All the cool kids are wearing these."

"Looks like the swelling has gone down, at least."

He nodded. "It has. I can open my eye halfway now, so that's an improvement." He shook the bottle of pills he had. "They gave a few pills for the pain and swelling. Said the meds might make me a little dizzy."

"No worries. I'll keep you upright." Laughing, she grabbed his hand. "Let's get you home."

She drove him across town to his complex in Virginia Highlands, then helped him up the stairs to his second-floor unit while lugging his bass behind her. Her free hand resting on his back, she applied gentle pressure as they ascended. "Careful, now."

He smiled. "I'm good." He inserted his key in the lock and let the door swing open.

She followed him inside, easing the bass around the door frame. "Where do want this?"

He gestured to the corner of the living room area. "Just set it in that black metal stand."

She passed him and deposited the instrument case in the designated spot. "Do you…think you'll be okay?" She looked at his face, then the front door, then set her gaze on him again.

"Yes." Swollen eye be damned, he wouldn't let this moment pass. "But I'd be better if you stayed."

Ten

Teagan felt the smile curl her lips in response to his softly spoken invitation. "You really want me to stay?"

He nodded. "Only if you want to. If you're uncomfortable, just say so and I'll take my bruised eye and go to bed, alone." He grinned.

She laughed. Feeling the boldness rise within, she eased closer to him. "I'd like to stay, Maxton."

He closed the distance between them and pulled her into his arms.

For a moment, they just stood there, holding each other. Teagan felt the warmth of his body against hers, and it felt safe. It felt right.

He stepped away and led her by the hand to the

sofa. "Do you…wanna watch TV? Or hear some music?" He sat down and tugged her hand.

Sinking into the soft cushion, she cozied up to his side and kicked off her gold pumps. "Music, please."

He turned on the television and flipped to a satellite music station playing classic soul and R & B. An old Isley Brothers tune filled the room. "How's that?"

"Good." She smiled, resting her head on his shoulder. "Now that we're settled, I wanna hear the story behind that new earring."

"Yesterday was my sister's birthday." He sighed. "After the session, I spent a lot of time sitting here alone, feeling the weight of my sadness. I video chatted with my mom. After a while, I started to get restless, you know. So I decided to go do something in her memory, and I already had a tattoo." He touched the tiny letter, and it dangled. "This was the next thing I could think of."

"I like it. It's not too big, and it fits your style." She paused. "What's your happiest memory with your sister?"

"Odd question, but an easy answer." He let his head drop back against the sofa cushion. "Back when she was a senior in high school, she won homecoming queen. Even though it's tradition for the winner's dad to walk the queen across the field, she asked me to do it. I drove home from USC. She was so beautiful in that gold-sequined dress, and the cheers were so loud from the stands."

She felt the smile tugging at her lips and her heart. "That's so sweet."

"I can still hear them chanting her name. Yeah. I was so proud of her and so honored that she chose me." He gazed straight ahead as if replaying the moments in his mind. "Afterwards, I asked her why she asked me instead of dad. She said 'because you understand me better than anybody and I look up to you.'"

"That's really beautiful."

"You know, she would've turned twenty-seven yesterday." The darkness of his pain threatened to rise again, but he forced it down. "I just wish… I wish things could be different."

She sensed there was something more, something he was holding back, but she didn't want to press him. The last thing she wanted to do was intensify his grief. "You know, my grandmother used to tell me that no one ever really dies as long as they're remembered in love." She touched his face, gliding her palm along his cheek. "Whitney lives, Maxton. Right here." She moved her palm down his upper body until it rested against the center of his chest.

He swallowed, and his eyes glistened.

"I can see now that your music, your beautiful artistry, has been forged in the fire of pain. You're so strong, in ways you don't even realize."

His eyes locked with hers as he raised his hand, cupping her cheek. "That may be true. But I'm not strong enough to fight off what I'm feeling right now."

Her tongue darted out to sweep across her lower lip.

"Will you let me make love to you tonight, Teagan?"

Her pulse quickened; her nipples bloomed. "Yes."

He smiled and tilted her face to his liking before pressing his lips to hers. The moment their mouths connected, she felt the arousal shoot through her body like an electric current. She opened her mouth and his tongue slipped inside to twist against her own. Soon, he drew her into his lap, and she went willingly, giving herself over to him without hesitation.

His hands caressed her fevered skin as he kissed her, moving from her lips to the hollow of her neck, to her collarbone. He placed a sultry lick along the line of her cleavage, and she sighed aloud.

When he pulled back, he tugged the hem of her top and she raised her arms, allowing him to take it off and toss it aside. He kissed along the scalloped edge of her bra while simultaneously reaching behind her to undo the hooks. As her breasts bounced free, he growled before closing his mouth over one aching, hardened nipple.

Her head dropped back, and she moaned as he licked and sucked, enthralled by the searing pleasure of his warm mouth. He switched to the other nipple and gave it the same loving attention, and her back arched in response. "Oh, Maxton."

His face buried between her breasts, he murmured, "You like that?"

"Mmm."

"Then, you'll love what's next." He eased her off his lap, kneeling on the floor in front of her.

She trembled as he slid his large hands over her, gliding from her ankle up to her knee. There, he lingered on the hem of her black A-line skirt. "Open for me, shorty."

She widened her legs, and the trembling increased while he made slow, small circles along her inner thighs. Tugging her panties to the side, he slipped beneath the fabric and she shuddered at the first contact of his fingertips against her womanly heat.

He swirled his fingers around the already tight bud of her clitoris, and she could hear her own rapid breathing. When he dipped one long finger inside, her moans rose, drowning out the music.

"So wet," he mumbled as he tugged at her waistband.

She lifted her hips, allowing him to free her from the panties. Moments later, he draped one of her legs over the arm of the sofa and leaned into her. The moment his hot mouth came into contact with her sex, she cried out.

He swept his tongue through her folds, tasting her, worshipping her, and she could feel the power of ecstasy rising within. She widened her legs, her hands gripping the soft curls at the back of his head, and pulled him in, craving more even as he drove her closer to madness.

He growled into her as he pushed his tongue inside her and she screamed as a warm gush spurted from her. He eased back, licking his lips. "So, you, uh…"

"Yeah," she said breathlessly. "I did."

"I'll take that as a compliment." He grinned broadly.

She stared at the shine still lingering on his lips and felt her pulse pounding all over again. Her body still humming, she was barely aware of him sliding a tray from beneath the sofa, then sliding it back. "What is it?" He asked.

She parted her lips to say two simple words. "Get naked."

He did as she asked, stripping off his black sneakers, tee, jeans and the designer boxers beneath, with his back to her. She heard the crinkle of a foil packet, and he turned around as he finished rolling on the protection. Her eyes widened when she saw his dick, hard and sheathed in black. She wrapped her hands around the thickness for a moment, giving it a gentle squeeze. "Sit down."

Once he was seated, she straddled him and used her hand to guide him inside. They groaned together as he filled her, and her internal walls expanded, then contracted to welcome him. She circled her hips, treating him to a slow ride while his big hands gripped her hips. Her fingertips dug into his strong shoulders, giving her leverage as she continued to grind against him, feeling the growing swell of pleasure. She picked up her pace, leaning forward and moving her hips up and down like a piston, racing toward the orgasm she felt building in her belly.

"Shit!" The bubble burst, and her being shattered into light and brilliance.

"Teagan," he rasped, and his body stiffened beneath her as he found release.

She leaned forward, resting against him and enjoying the feeling of simply being held in his arms. He remained inside her, and just as the post-lovemaking drowsiness began to take hold, she felt him thickening and growing again. "Maxton?"

"Looks like we need to take this party to the bedroom." He gave her ass a firm squeeze before scooting forward and standing. Instinctively, she wrapped her legs around his waist and tightened her grasp on his shoulders. He began walking with her in his arms, but soon her back came to rest against the wall.

"Just one more time," he said throatily as he began to pump, "then I'll take you to bed."

Her eyes rolled back as he stroked the fire inside her once again.

Later, as they lay, spent and sweat-dampened in his bed, she whispered, "You have even more talents than I thought."

He chuckled in the darkness. "And you still haven't experienced them all."

She took a deep breath, settling into his arms. *Yes,*

*this little arrangement could lead to a lot of fun...
if we do everything just right.* To that end, she said,
"I'll have to leave pretty early in the morning since
I have to go home, get a shower and all that."

"I get it. And I'll wait to hear from you, to see
when we'll start recording again." He yawned. "It's
all good."

"Thanks." She was glad he seemed to understand
the importance of discretion, and that he didn't make
a big deal of it.

Yes. This was going to be a lot of fun.

Taking a sip from the cup of chamomile tea in his
hand, Maxton looked at the circle of metal folding
chairs beyond him in the meeting room of Neal Wellness Center. Once he'd finished the tea, he tossed the
foam cup into the trash can, then settled onto the seat
of an empty chair. Immediately, the coolness snaked
across the back of his thighs, a stark contrast to the
mid-July heat outside that had driven him to dress
in shorts. Looking around at the small circle of men,
he thought back to last week's meeting, which had
been his first, and tried to place names with the faces
surrounding him.

He could remember two of the other four men
present: Bill, who was in his early forties, had a kind
face and ice-blue eyes. Kip, the youngest of the group
at only nineteen, had brown hair with frosted blond
tips and wore a leather jacket and matching pants
despite the intense heat of a Georgia summer lurk-

ing just beyond the building's doors. *How does he wear that this time of year without passing out?* He wasn't particularly fond of summer, because he felt his style was best expressed in darker clothing that covered more skin. However, there was only so far he would go in the name of fashion. At some point, practicality had to come into play.

The other two men, he remembered their stories rather than their names. One, an older Black man, had lost a mother to a tragic robbery-turned-murder, and the other had spoken about his daughter's unfortunate death after a night of drinking. He assumed everyone present was a patient of his therapist, but he didn't know that for sure and didn't feel it was his place to ask. Besides, how they came to attend the meetings didn't matter. They were all here for the same reasons: to heal, and to grow.

The room's door swung open, and Dr. Alan Tyndall entered, carrying his clipboard case. A Black man in his early sixties, he had a short graying Afro and a mustache. He wore black slacks, a white button-down and a simple red tie. "Good evening, everybody." As the therapist took the last empty seat in the circle, everyone exchanged greetings.

Dr. Tyndall had been Maxton's therapist for the past six months, having worked with him in teletherapy while he was out touring with various musical artists. Now that he was in Atlanta for a time, Dr. Tyndall had suggested Maxton join his small support group, Men Managing Loss.

"So, gentlemen, who would like to be the first to share this week?" Dr. Tyndall let his gaze touch each face in the group and waited for a few moments. When no one volunteered, he pointed to Bill. "Bill, why don't you tell us how your week went?"

Bill drew a deep breath, clasping his hands together. "It's been three years now since I lost Ida in that car accident, so that means I made it to another milestone." He paused. "I also…think I might be ready to try dating again."

The other men offered smiles and words of encouragement; Bill's responding smile was a bit crooked but genuine.

"That's wonderful, Bill. What brought this on?" Dr. Tyndall leaned forward. "Was there any particular thing this week that gave you the final push?"

He nodded. "I was talking to my sister-in-law, and she told me for the umpteenth time that Ida wouldn't want me isolating like this. She'd want me to move on. But I think this time when she said it, I was finally ready to hear her."

"That's a very encouraging sign of growth, Bill. Is there anything else you'd like to share?"

Bill shook his head. "That's all for me."

"Maxton? How about you?" Dr. Tyndall looked his way. "I see your eye has healed up."

Maxton nodded. "Yeah. Well, we're on the eighth song of that album at work. We had to take two days off because of that incident, but I think we're back on track now."

Dr. Tyndall nodded, resting the eraser end of his pencil against his chin. "That's good to hear. But I'm curious to know how you're dealing with the mental and emotional aftermath of that incident."

Maxton swallowed. "I guess I'm doing alright. I mean, it's been hard to focus in the studio at times. We haven't had any more problems. Swagg isn't going to allow any more guests in there during our sessions."

"That's good, but it's less about what's happening in the studio now and more about how you're processing the underlying emotions brought on by what happened."

"It's hard to explain. But I…get angry, almost irrationally so, when I'm by myself." Maxton folded his hands into his lap. "I mean, it just pisses me off. How could a man even think it's okay to just swing on a woman like that? I had to stop him. I had to…" He stopped, midsentence, as realization hit.

"What?" Dr. Tyndall pressed. "What did you have to do, Maxton?"

"I had to protect her."

"Why?" He narrowed his eyes, the way he often did when analyzing what he heard.

The lump formed in his throat, and he felt his shoulders slump. "Because I couldn't protect Whitney. And I just couldn't bear failing again." He folded his arms over his chest, angry that he couldn't stop the tears.

"Whoa. Major breakthrough, my guy." Kip whistled.

"You're safe here, brother," another man added. "I wrestled with that guilt after I lost my little girl to alcohol poisoning. I beat myself up for months, wondering if there was somewhere I went wrong. I worried that I should have made her go to college closer to home or checked up on her more, anything that would have kept her away from that damn fraternity kegger." He shook his head.

"I've journeyed through the valley of guilt myself, Maxton." Dr. Tyndall straightened, tenting his fingers. "I'm a therapist. Mental health and wellness are my life. Yet I lost my own wife to suicide. I should have been better equipped than anyone to help her, to save her. But sometimes, life simply doesn't give us that chance."

Looking around at the faces of these men, of varying ages and from all different backgrounds, Maxton felt seen, heard, understood. Their shared experience of grief and loss, of powerlessness and regret had brought them all to this small room inside a nondescript building in Midtown. And though his journey in the group, and in a way, through his grief, had just begun, he felt grateful for them, nonetheless.

"We've all gone through some form of guilt," Bill stated solemnly. "I gotta tell you, it's a dead-end street. Nothing good can come of it."

Running his hand over his head, Maxton sighed. "When I remember that moment when the zip-line equipment malfunctioned, and I heard her scream... I just can't help wishing I could have stopped it from happening. I would even have taken my sister's place. But since I couldn't do that, I'm just...stuck. Stuck with the guilt, the pain, the sadness that seems like it will eat me alive sometimes."

"Thank you for your honesty, Maxton." Dr. Tyndall crossed his legs. "I think this is a good place to remind ourselves that there are two useless emotions— guilt and shame. These are the feelings that feed off the darkness inside of us, then use those regrets against us, to tell us that we aren't enough. But that's not true. We are enough."

The men around the circle nodded and murmured their agreement.

"And beyond that, we must make friends with time. As it passes, it naturally facilitates our healing. Let go of the worry that you'll forget your loved one. They were much too important for that. The mark they left on your lives is a legacy, something you can share and pass on to others. Tell your children about them. Tell your neighbors and friends about the lives they lived. Do good works in their name. Let the love you have for them stamp out the pain and the guilt, and let the joy of knowing they were a part of your life override all else." Dr. Tyndall let a small smile tug his lips. "My work in my wife's name is here, in this group. Have you ever read the sign above the door of this room?"

Most of them shook their heads.

His smile broadened. "This is the Elise Valmont Tyndall Room for Restoration and Recovery.

I funded this space in her honor, to create a safe place for men to heal from loss. And this work, as hard as it is sometimes, fills me up with something I can hardly describe. And it leaves very little room for guilt."

When the meeting ended, Maxton hung back. "Dr. Tyndall, can I ask a quick question?"

"Go ahead." He snapped his clipboard case shut, resting it in the crook of his elbow.

"I'm not sure what my work will be. You know, the thing I do in Whitney's honor."

"You're already in a creative profession," the therapist pointed out. "Why not think of ways you can use your talent to honor her and perhaps help others in her memory?"

He nodded. "I'll think about that. Thanks, Doc."

"No problem." He patted him on the shoulder. "I'm sure you'll come up with something."

Eleven

Thursday afternoon, Teagan was back at the workstation for day sixteen of recording Lil Swagg's album. And based on the expression on the young rapper's face, the workday would soon come to an end.

The musicians were now recording their fifth iteration of the album's eighth track, and she could tell that everyone's patience was thin at this point. Peering through the glass into the booth, she could see the tight expression on Maxton's face. Something was off about his playing, though she couldn't quite name it. Where he usually fingered his instrument deftly and smoothly, today, his movements seemed stiff, almost rote. His improvisations were almost absent, and his cadence was slightly skewed.

She sighed, thinking back on the last two weeks with him. They'd spent a good amount of time outside the studio together, hitting up the city's restaurants and taking long walks in the park. When they weren't out and about, they'd convened at his place for some smoking-hot sex. They kept their interactions professional at the studio, but when they were alone together, behind closed doors, all pretense was dropped as they gave in to the passion simmering between them.

Swagg rose from his seat on the sofa and came to stand next to her. "What is going on with them today?"

She shrugged. "I don't know. Something is definitely off, though."

"They usually sound so dope, but they don't really seem to be feelin' it today." He raised his index finger above his head, circling it around. "Yo, that's it. Cut the playback."

She tapped her screen, ceasing the stripped-down melody that the band members had been building around.

Swagg gestured to the intercom. "May I?"

"Sure. I'll press the button. You talk." She pressed the green button.

"Listen up, y'all. I don't know what the problem is, but y'all just not hittin' the mark today. So why don't we knock off early, y'all rest up, fill your well and whatnot, and just come back rested and ready to do this shit tomorrow? Everybody good with that?"

All four of them gave the thumbs-up.

"Cool."

Teagan pressed the red button to end his broadcast.

The booth's door opened with the musicians filing out. Maxton was last to leave.

"See you tomorrow," she called to him.

He glanced her way. "Yeah. You too."

She cringed inwardly, noting how his words lacked their usual warmth. *What's going on with him? Did I do or say something wrong?"*

Swagg stopped Maxton on the way out. "You good, homie? Because a track can live and die by the bass line, and you weren't at your best today."

Maxton nodded. "Yeah, I was just a little distracted. Got a lot on my mind." He hoisted his instrument case from one hand to the other. "I'm good, though. Tomorrow, I'll be ready."

Swagg waved. "See you tomorrow."

"See ya." Maxton turned and walked out.

While Swagg and Rick gathered their things, Teagan tried to focus on making sure today's work was properly saved and cataloged, but her mind kept going to Maxton. If he were her man, she'd have every right to follow him and press him for answers about whatever seemed to be bothering him.

But he's not my man. This is a fling. No strings attached, not even if I'm concerned. She simply didn't have a leg to stand on, because keeping things casual had been her idea in the first place. If she started making exceptions to their agreement now, who knew where it would lead. Probably not anywhere she was ready to go. So she pushed the thoughts away.

Left alone in the studio after Swagg and Rick's exit, she ended her session and set the workstation in shutdown mode. While she waited for the on-screen prompts to indicate the process was finished, she heard the echoing sound of someone shouting in the hallway. Considering her encounter with Money J and his thugs a couple of weeks ago, she didn't want to wait and see what the source of the sound was. At least Vic Grip, while misguided in his decision to bring the other men to her studio, had been gentlemanly enough not to participate in their childish brawl.

Rising from her seat, she went to the studio door and peered down the hall.

There was her father, walking in her direction from the elevator bank. He was shouting into his cell phone, and she immediately became curious as to why. It wasn't like her father to do something so unprofessional in a public space, so she assumed it was something pretty serious.

She turned back to see the screen go black on the workstation, then grabbed her purse and keys. Locking the door behind her, she headed toward her father, who'd now stopped in the hallway to carry on his angry phone conversation.

"No! Don't you dare come here. You won't be

allowed on the premises!" His face twisted into a scowl; he stabbed the air with his finger. "Now, you listen, and you listen good. I don't know how you got my number, but don't you ever call me again. And don't come anywhere near me or my family, or I will have you arrested!" He took the phone away from his ear and jabbed the screen to end the call.

She looked at her father's untied necktie, sweat-dampened brow and his flashing eyes, wondering what was going on. Soon, though, she remembered. "Was that him, Dad? The man that claims you're his father?"

"Yes, that was that lying miscreant." He stuffed the phone into his pocket and marched past her.

She followed him into the security office directly adjacent to the reception desk. Only one officer was currently on duty, and he looked up from the camera monitors as soon as they entered.

"Mr. Woodson, is there a problem?"

"Owen, I need you to implement a one hundred percent ID check on anyone entering this building. If they're not staff or a member of the Woodson family, check their identification. I don't want anyone with the last name Woodbine on 404 Sound property, for any reason."

"Yes, sir. I'll take care of it right now." Owen spun his chair from the security monitor to the computer and began typing.

Teagan backed out of the way as her father exited the security office, then followed him as he stalked through the main door of the building. "Dad, slow down."

He stopped on the sidewalk and looked at her. "What is it, Teagan? Can't you see I'm in the middle of something?"

"Yes, and it looks like that something is a nervous breakdown." She shook her head. "Dad, you know I love you so, so much. But I tried to tell you that this guy wasn't going to stop."

He grimaced as if hearing her words caused him physical pain. "Please spare me the I-told-you-so, child. My pressure is already up."

She rested her hand on his forearm, giving it a gentle squeeze through the fabric of his light blue button-down. "What did he say to you that got you so upset, Dad?"

"He just restated the same lie that he wrote in that letter. The only difference is, he claims to have proof."

She stilled. "Proof?" That was a pretty bold claim to make, especially since her father was so insistent that there was no veracity to the claim. "That's… troubling."

He huffed. "It's absurd, that's what it is. None of this is true, so the proof he's talking about doesn't even exist or is faked." He shook his head solemnly. "Whoever this young man is, he missed his calling as an actor."

She asked the question that to her seemed the

next most logical. "Okay. Now that you see this isn't going away, are you going to talk to Mom about it?"

He sighed. "Why must you keep bringing your mother into this? I've already told you this is all some elaborate lie. Why should I drag her into this, knowing she'd be just as upset as I am? I'd rather spare Addy this nonsense."

Teagan sucked in a breath. "Yes, I'm sure Mom would be upset to learn about this. But can you imagine how absolutely livid she'd be if she heard it from someone other than you?"

He frowned. "How would that happen, Teagan? You, me and Gloria are the only ones who know. My secretary knows better, and so do you." He looked at her pointedly. "Don't interfere with this, Teagan. This is my issue, and I'm going to handle it as I see fit."

She released his arm. "Dad, I'm not going to go behind your back. But I am gonna keep nudging you to tell Mom about this. Please. We don't know what this guy is capable of."

He hesitated, and she saw the contemplation play across his face. "I'll think about it."

"That's all I ask." She pecked him on the cheek. "Love you, Daddy."

"I love you too, baby girl." With a forlorn smile, he turned and walked to his car.

As she got into her own car, Teagan couldn't help thinking of Maxton again. Part of her wanted to call him, wanted to ask what she should do about this whole mess with her father. She didn't like keeping secrets from her mother, but she also didn't want to break her word.

She grabbed her phone out of her purse to call Maxton but stopped short. After the way he'd acted toward her today, she had no reason to believe he'd be interested in hearing about her problems. Besides, that would probably exceed the parameters of their little fling.

She put her phone away and started the engine. As she pulled out of the parking lot, she couldn't help thinking of how this thing seemed determined to outgrow the box they'd tried to put it in.

Sitting on his sofa, Maxton used his small laptop to perform an internet search. Dr. Tyndall's advice had been bouncing around in his head for a couple of days now, and he wanted to go ahead and make some moves toward building something meaningful in Whitney's name.

Ever since the seed had been planted in his mind, he'd been thinking about it. Admittedly, his preoccupation with this new mission had contributed to his less-than-stellar playing in the recording session today. *I don't want that to happen again, so I need to get this together so I can concentrate on my work.*

He wasn't going to rush the process, not with something as precious as his sister's legacy at stake. What he needed was a firm plan, a solid foundation.

Once he had that in place, he knew he could go back to putting his heart and soul into his current gig.

He clicked on a link to the home page of a website explaining how to form a nonprofit organization. He leaned back against the cushions, slowly scrolling as he read the information on the screen. *Damn, this is a lot. Better take some notes.* He opened a text file, snapped the two windows next to each other, and typed up a few pertinent items.

The sound of someone knocking at his door drew his attention. Setting the laptop aside, he stood and went to answer it, expecting some salesperson or a local churchgoer passing out tracts.

As he checked the peephole, he got a surprise. Opening the door, he said, "Teagan? What are you doing here?"

Still dressed in the knee-length purple sheath she'd worn at the studio earlier, she offered him a crooked smile. "I was going to call, but… I thought this would be better."

"Um…" he glanced at his computer, then back to her. *She did drive all the way over here… I guess my planning session will have to wait.* He took a big step back. "Come on in."

"Thanks." She entered and closed the door behind her. "I hope I'm not interrupting anything."

He jogged over to the sofa and shut his laptop. "I was just poking around online. So, what brings you here?"

She approached him and dropped her handbag

on the coffee table, her hand coming up to stroke his jawline. "I just…really need a distraction right now." She grabbed his hand, moving it to her thigh and curling his fingers around the hem of her dress. "Do you think you can help me out?"

He swallowed, looking down into her sultry eyes. "Yeah."

"Good." She gave him a peck on the cheek, then turned away from him.

He felt his brow furrow, but confusion quickly turned to arousal when he saw what she was doing. She kicked off her sandals, went to the arm of the sofa and bent over it.

Blood surged into his dick at the sight of her up-turned hips. No woman had ever approached him so boldly, and he'd never been this turned on. As he palmed her ass through the thin fabric of her dress, she widened her stance.

"Please, Maxton. I need it," she crooned, her voice low and sultry.

He quickly grabbed a condom from the secret drawer under the sofa, snatched down his shorts and boxers, and sheathed himself. That done, he lifted her dress, bunching the fabric around her waist. Hooking his thumbs under the band of her lacy black bikini underwear, he dragged them down her legs and watched her step out of them.

He licked his lips, anticipating the feel of her as he rested one hand on the small of her back. Using his other hand, he guided himself inside her tightness.

"Oh, yes," she purred, as he reached the deepest part of her.

He began his work then, at first using a gentle, slow stroke that tested the limits of his self-control. He gripped her waist, drawing her body in closer to his with each thrust. Her soft moans filled his ears, spurring him on.

Soon, keeping his pace slow became impossible, and he sped up to match the desire roaring through his body like wildfire. The pitch of her moans changed, growing higher as he put even more power into the movements of his hips. Her body, so wet and tight, threatened to drain him of every ounce of strength he had, but he didn't care. Nothing mattered but her cries of ecstasy and the release he felt building inside.

She screamed as her body clenched around him. That was enough to push him over the edge, and moments later, he felt his own body pulsing inside her as he came. He eased away from her, disposed of the condom, then returned and slipped back into his boxers.

As she stood, tugging down her dress, she giggled.

He raised a brow. "That's not a critique of my performance, is it?"

"Of course not. You were amazing." She shook her head, still laughing. "I just can't believe I did that. I must really be stressed-out."

He chuckled as he flopped down on the sofa. "I

guess so." Patting his lap, he said, "Sit down. Tell me what's on your mind."

She sat on his lap sideways and settled into his embrace with a sigh. "Look, Maxton. I know this thing between us is all about keeping it light, no strings, all of that. But I'm sitting on a huge secret, and I don't really have anyone else I can unburden myself to."

"Nobody?"

She shook her head. "Miles and Nia are family, so they can't know. And unfortunately, I don't really have any close friends, just acquaintances." She inhaled deeply. "A lot of that is my fault. I'm probably the least social of all the Woodson kids."

"Okay." He scratched his chin, wondering what was bothering her so much. "Let me guess. This has something to do with your Dad?"

"Yes. That situation I told you about before. It's back, just like I said it would be."

"Are you going to tell me what this 'situation' is, Teagan?"

She nodded. "I will if you promise me you won't tell anyone else."

"I won't." He held up his hand. "I don't have any reason to go telling your family's business."

"A young man has come forward, claiming that he's my father's illegitimate son."

His eyes grew wide. "Oh, snap."

"Yeah. My father denies the whole thing, even going so far as to say it's impossible that this person is his child. But he won't let up. First, he sent that letter a couple of weeks ago. Then, a few hours ago, he called my dad's cell phone to make the same claim directly to him."

"That seems like more of your dad's problem than yours. So why are you so upset?"

"For starters, the mere existence of this accusation has shaken my view of the man I thought my father was. But the absolute worst part is that my father refuses to tell my mother about it, so she's totally in the dark about this whole mess." She shook her head. "And that puts me in the very awkward position of lying to my mother. It isn't a position I want to be in."

"That's…a lot. I can see why you'd be stressed-out by it." He ran his hand over her hair, playing with the few tendrils that had escaped her low bun. "So, what are you going to do?"

She shrugged. "Nothing, right now. I told Dad I wouldn't say anything to Mom. But I just know this is gonna blow up in his face, and I told him as much."

"Then, there's really not much you can do."

"I guess you're right." She cupped his face in her hands. "Telling you did help, though. So thanks for listening."

"You're welcome." He gave her a soft, gentle kiss on the lips.

Looking at her, so comfortable in his arms, made him think very seriously about their arrangement. The more time he spent with her, the more he felt his heart opening to her. They'd begun with a promise to keep things casual, to keep things fun. Now here he was, reconsidering the very foundation of what they'd agreed to.

His feelings for her were growing, and if she could trust him enough to share with him what she just had, he may as well take a chance and trust her with what he felt. There was something between them, something real, something works more than a fling.

"Teagan, I need to tell you something."

"Go ahead. I'm listening."

"I've been thinking we should…" The sound of the alarm on his phone going off interrupted him, and he cursed, remembering. "Shit."

"What's wrong?"

He shifted, scooting from beneath her. "It's almost six, and I have an appointment."

The corners of her mouth fell, and her shoulders drooped. "Do you have to go?"

He nodded as he stepped into his shorts and dragged them up. "Yeah, I do. It's really important. I'm sorry to rush you off. It's just that when you—" he pointed to the sofa arm "—did that, I totally forgot about it."

"I can see how that could happen." She sighed but got up and slipped back into her panties and shoes. "I'll let you go. See you tomorrow at the studio."

"Yep. See you there." He pulled his shirt over his head and tugged the tail down.

She gave him a quick peck on the cheek, grabbed her purse and left.

A few minutes later, he grabbed his wallet and the keys to his rental and ran out the door.

Twelve

"So, it's true, then. You and the bassist?"

Teagan shook her head in response to her older sister's voice coming over her car's speakers. "I thought we were being discreet, but I guess not."

"Come on, Teagan. 404 is a family-owned business. You know how fast word gets around the building." She chuckled. "I gotta admit I'm surprised. I didn't think you had it in you to have a fling."

"I didn't, either." She thought back to last night, and how quickly passion had turned to awkwardness. "It's funny, though. Just when people start talking about our little arrangement, things get weird between us."

Nia sounded confused. "What do you mean?"

She signed. "I went over there yesterday to…hang

out. Anyway, when we were just chilling on the sofa, his phone went off and he jumped up, saying he had an appointment. Then he basically put me out so he could go."

"What's weird about that? Maybe he really had an appointment."

"Maybe, but that's not the issue." She turned right, onto the side street where 404's building was located. "Just before the phone went off, he got this really serious look on his face and started to tell me something. When he jumped up to get ready, he never finished his sentence."

"He didn't call or text you last night to clear things up?"

"Nope. So now I'm just left wondering what he was going to say." She shrugged, pulling into her designated parking space. "I'm gonna see him shortly, so I suppose I can just ask."

"Hmm. You'd better brace for impact."

"Why?" She cut the engine, switching her phone to speaker mode, and reached into the passenger seat for her purse.

"You say he had a serious look on his face. What if he wanted to end things and was trying to let you down gently or something?"

Teagan felt a twinge in her chest at her sister's words. As much as she didn't want to think about it, she'd started to get attached to Maxton in a way she hadn't intended. "Who knows what was on his mind? I just wish he'd said it, so I wouldn't have to be worried about it now." She blew out a breath. "With Swagg's album and everything going on with Dad…" She clapped her hand over her mouth, but it was already too late.

"Yeah, what's up with Dad? He's been a little extra salty lately."

"I, uh, nothing," she stammered. "Listen, I'm here. So I gotta go."

"Teagan, wait—"

She disconnected the call. *Yikes. I can't believe I slipped up like that.* As she reached for the door handle, she glanced in the rearview and saw Maxton's rented convertible pull into the lot. Getting out of the car, she walked down the sidewalk toward the right side of the building where he'd parked.

The air felt hot and sticky, despite the early hour. She'd dressed in lighter colors, donning a yellow pencil skirt with a striped, yellow-and-white button-down blouse and nude pumps, in an attempt to reflect rather than absorb the searing Georgia sunshine. Her heels clicked on the concrete as she moved toward her objective: answers.

Moments later, she met him near the southeast corner of the building.

Dressed in denim shorts that revealed his hard thighs, a black polo and black sneakers, he wore a thick silver chain with a three-dimensional skull pendant dangling from his neck. Dark sunglasses over his eyes, he gripped the handle to his instrument case as he strode toward her. "Good morning."

"Morning." She eyed him. "This is a pretty tame look for you."

He shrugged. "I agree. But it's getting too hot for the kind of stuff I like to wear."

"I see." She paused. "Before we go inside, can I ask you something?"

"Sure. What's up?"

"What were you going to say to me last night? You know, before you had to rush off to that appointment?"

He sucked in his lower lip. "Yeah, again, I'm sorry I had to run out the way I did. You were…very distracting."

She offered him a small smile. "I figure it must have been important. Anyway, it's fine. I just wanted you to finish saying whatever it was you started to say before you left."

He shifted his weight, looked away. "I…don't think this is a good time to talk about that."

Her sister's warning echoed in her ear, and she bristled. "Oh, so it's like that? Are you at least going to tell me where you went in such a hurry last night?"

He titled his head to one side. "Not that I owe you an explanation, but I have a standing Thursday-night therapy session."

She frowned, narrowing her eyes. "I never said you owed me anything, I simply asked a question. I'm just trying to get a little clarity here."

"Clarity on what, exactly?" He rested his free

hand on his waist. "Why would you even care where I went?"

Noticing the change in his stance, she said, "Wait a minute, Maxton. I don't like your tone."

"You don't like my tone? Really?" His lips curled into a sarcastic smile. "That's rich, considering your tone right now, not to mention how you just showed up at my apartment yesterday unannounced. Not even a text to let me know you were on your way."

"I asked if I was interrupting, and…"

"No." He cut her off. "I may have been raised in Cali, but I know it's rude to just dismiss a visitor. So I wasn't going to just dismiss you, the way you dismissed my time and convenience by showing up the way you did."

She stared. "I'm sorry. I didn't realize I'd inconvenienced you. I didn't hear any complaints when you were making love to me." She cringed, realizing she should have left that last part as interior monologue, but she couldn't unsay it now.

His brow creased; his jaw hardened. "You know, you're a real piece of work. You insisted from the beginning that we keep this thing casual…"

Teagan heard the telltale creak of the side door being opened but didn't turn toward the sound.

"Yet you appear at my home, distract me from what I was working on, then proceed to drop this whole mess with your dad's outside child in my lap…"

"What outside kid?"

Teagan's heart dropped so fast, she was sure it bounced off the pavement. Turning toward the door, she saw her mother standing there, a few feet away. She must have just exited the building from the side door.

Addison, dressed in a bright red pantsuit with her hair up in a high chignon, walked a few steps closer to her daughter. "Teagan, what is he talking about? What's going on?"

Glancing back at Maxton, she gritted out, "Thanks a lot."

He rolled his eyes. "Shit! I'm going inside. The session is gonna start soon." He strode past her and went around to the front of the building.

Teagan didn't know if he went that way because he always entered through the front or because he didn't want to get any closer to them.

Addison grabbed her daughter's hand. "Teagan, can you please tell me what the hell is going on? I clearly heard that young man say something about your father and an outside child!"

Squeezing her mother's hand, she said, "Mom, let's go inside to your office. I'll explain it to you there."

Entering through the side door, she popped her head inside Studio Two. Trevor, sitting at his old faithful soundboard, turned around when she entered. "What's up, boss lady?"

"Can you get the session started in Studio One, please? I need like half an hour."

"I gotcha covered." The longtime employee glanced between their two faces. "Everything alright?"

"That remains to be seen," Addison said.

"Thanks, Trevor. I'll be back ASAP."

She and her mother boarded the elevator, taking it to the fourth floor. There, Addison let Teagan into her office. As Teagan sat down, Addison closed the door behind her.

"Are you going to tell me what's going on now?" Addison sat on the edge of her desk.

She looked up at her mother, towering over her due to her position, and had a flashback to her days as a little kid. Back then, her mother had seemed like a superwoman. But today, with the worry and concern lining her face, Teagan could see that her mother wasn't nearly as impervious to damage as she'd once thought. "I can't, Mom."

Folding her arms over her chest, she asked, "And why not?"

"I gave Dad my word that I wouldn't speak to you about this." She drew a deep breath. "My best advice is to just go talk to him."

Addison sighed. "I just can't believe this is happening. I'm walking out for a coffee run, and I overhear you arguing with..." She paused. "Wait a minute. Why were you two arguing? Isn't he one of the musicians working on that album in your recording suite?"

She nodded. "Yes, he is."

Addison rolled her eyes. "You know what? Never mind. I don't have the mental capacity to handle whatever you've got going on on top of what I just overheard." She stood, pacing the room's hardwood floor, her heels clicking in time. "Did I hear it right? Please tell me I'm mistaken."

"I can't do that, Mom." She rested her cheek in her hand. "Please, just go talk to Dad. I'm already way more involved in this than I ever wanted to be." *If only Gloria had just handed over that letter, maybe I could have avoided getting ensnared in this whole enterprise.*

"Don't you worry. I'm going to Caleb's office right now and getting some answers, straight from the source." Addison opened her office door. "Go on downstairs and handle the session. I'll deal with your father."

Cringing inwardly, Teagan got up and left the room.

Max sat on the low stool in his corner of the booth, his bass across his lap. He'd practically slid into the room not too long ago, not wanting to hold up the recording session. In his haste to remove the instrument from its case, he'd accidentally knocked it out of tune.

He strummed each of the strings in turn, listening to each note as it reverberated through the booth. All four single notes sounded off, though in different ways. He didn't bother with chords right now, knowing they'd sound like a chorus of alley cats. *Better to just tune the thing than subject everybody in the booth to that noise.*

Opening up the smartphone tuning app made by his bass manufacturer, he began the process of getting her back in tune. Left-handed guitarists were a rarity, and every time he took his bass in his hands, he remembered how hard it had been for him to learn to properly tune and play his instrument. With his left hand on the strings and his right hand on the tuners, he played the notes one by one. The E and A notes were sharp, while the D and G were both flat. Following the on-screen prompts, he loosened the first two tuners, then tightened the last two. With that done, he closed the app.

"Hey, Brady," he called.

"Yeah?" The guitarist turned his way.

"Can you give me a little Deep Purple, so I can test my tune?" He readied his fingers.

"No prob. First tune I ever learned how to play." Brady strapped on his guitar, a B.C. Rich Warlock Extreme edition in rich black lacquer, and began to play the famous opening stanza of the British rock band's hit "Smoke on the Water." Maxton picked up the bass line at the appropriate moment, and soon, the entire band was running through the 1972 classic. Mike used his keyboard to simulate the vocals, and the vibe was definitely there. They were all along for the ride, grooving, caught up in the magic of a familiar yet extraordinary piece of music. Four musicians, four instruments, all combining to create one awesome sound.

Swagg switched on the intercom as they wrapped up. "Yo, that was hot. Seems like y'all back in top form."

He hoped the rapper was right because he was determined to make up for the previous day's lack of progress. Swagg had given them an ambitious goal. Maxton wanted them to succeed in meeting it. *Challenge is good for a musician. It keeps you focused, keeps you learning, keeps complacency away.*

He was too young and too early in his career to start resting on his laurels. He wanted to always be learning, always be growing as a bassist. And in order to do that, he had to take the hard gigs, put in the long hours, play the pieces that made him nervous or fell outside his comfort zone.

Trevor, seated behind the workstation, held up his hand. "Let's pick up where you left off and run through track eight." Playback on the melody track started, and Maxton began picking out a bass line.

The rest of the band joined in, and Maxton felt the synergy inside the booth growing. He added a little flair to his line as the track reached its bridge, then eased up for the return to the chorus and the next eight bars. As the song's final eight bars played, he kicked it up another notch. The rest of the band followed his lead. Each musician added their own special touch to the combined sound. The music swelled, and the track ended with a rich, intense finish.

Swagg clapped his hands, nodding his approval as he reengaged the intercom. "Hell, yeah! That's what I'm talking about, y'all." He eased over to Trevor, touching his shoulder. "That's a wrap on that song, homie. I'm ready to get in the booth and lay my verses down."

Trevor nodded, and Swagg stepped into the booth. Maxton and the other musicians sat down on their stools and listened while he rapped his verses over their newly created track. Maxton bobbed his head in time, enjoying the way the music and Swagg's vocals blended together, complementing each other so well, with neither element overpowering the other.

As Swagg went into the song's bridge, the suite door swung open and Teagan walked in.

Maxton felt the smile slip from his face as he took in her gloomy expression. *Boy. I laid a big-ass egg with her today.* She looked stressed-out, and because of his careless blunder earlier, he knew he was to blame for that, at least partly.

Maxton watched Teagan for a few minutes as Swagg finished his vocals, and it soon became obvious that she refused to look in his direction. When they convened work on the album's ninth track, he found it difficult to regain the focus and flow he'd had just a short time earlier. His fingers slipped a few times, screwing up his chords and throwing off the cadence of the rest of the band.

Even as things inside the booth started to go to the

left, Teagan's gaze remained locked on her screen. She never looked up, not even a glance.

Swagg held up his hand, extended his index finger and swirled it around his head. Teagan gave him a subtle nod, then restarted playback on track nine's melody.

Once again, Maxton couldn't find his groove. He looked down at his fingers, minding their progress over the strings. But when he hazarded another glance at Teagan, he found her looking straight ahead through the glass. Her expression was one of utter boredom and disinterest.

Seeing that expression took him back to his days at Mrs. Hardy's Music Academy. He'd studied under her as a young, impressionable bassist, starting his lessons at the tender age of seven. His parents, while both scientists, had encourage his artistic interests and had paid the exorbitant fee allowing him to enter her elite academy. Years of absorbing his father's love of funk music, particularly the animated stylings of the legendary Bootsy Collins, had fueled Maxton's desire to play bass.

He'd taken lessons four days a week for ten years, completing Mrs. Hardy's Young Master's Program a few months before he started his senior year in high school. His parents, as well as his sister, Whitney, had praised his playing at every opportunity. But not Mrs. Hardy. While he was one of her star pupils, she rarely doled out praise. Even when she did, it usually came paired with some criticism or another. For years, he labored at improving his skills, filled with confidence and fear in equal measure.

She'd watch his recitals, stone-faced, as if she had somewhere else to be. And while her strict standards had helped him secure a spot at his dream school, he could still feel the sting of her disapproving stare whenever he made a mistake. This many years and this many miles away from Mrs. Hardy, he knew he shouldn't be feeling this way again.

Faltering beneath the weight of his frustration, he plucked his E string so hard, he snatched it right out of tune again. Even with the sounds of all the other instruments around him, he could hear how flat the note played. He cursed inwardly.

Sharrod dropped one of his drumsticks. As he snatched it up and started playing again, he glared at Maxton. "Get it together, bro!"

He did his best to salvage the piece, but his out-of-tune string made his bass line sound tinny and strange. He tried adjusting the tuning peg on the fly, but it just wasn't working.

Swagg gestured for them to stop, then spoke over the intercom. "You know what? Y'all slipping again. It's cool, though. We got a track done, so I'm good with reconvening Monday." Swagg looked pointedly from Teagan to Maxton. "Use the weekend to deal with whatever tension or hang-ups y'all might have. Because next week, we gon' blast through these last three tracks. Y'all feel me?"

Maxton swallowed. "Yeah." His bandmates offered their affirmatives as well, and he could feel their disapproving stares burning his face.

Teagan offered a tight nod.

"I'm glad we all on the same page. See y'all Monday." With that, Swagg departed.

Feeling chastised and embarrassed, Maxton settled onto the stool again and flipped open his instrument case, setting the bass inside. He snapped it shut and stayed seated as the other musicians packed up.

Sharrod eyed him. "Man, what's going on with you two? I told you this was a bad idea."

"Don't start with me, Sharrod." Taking in the tight set of this friend's face, he added, "I'll handle it. I promise."

"I hope so." Sharrod shoved his sticks into the back pocket of his jeans. "Because whatever you two have going, it's not cool to put the gig at risk for the rest of us." He turned and stalked out.

Alone in the booth, Maxton watched Teagan through the glass partition. She was still busying herself with anything else other than looking in his direction, but by now, he'd grown tired of it.

Getting his case, he left the booth, passed her in the outer suite and sat down on the sofa. "Teagan, can we talk about this?"

She ignored him, continuing to tap the touchscreen at the workstation.

He sighed. "Teagan, I know you can hear me."

Thirteen

Staring at the screen of her workstation, Teagan pretended there was no one else in the room. For a while it was easy, as she ran file cleanup and optimization on the track-eight audio they'd created today. She simply tuned out the insistent voice behind her, choosing instead to focus on the colored patterns flashing across the screen, tracking the process as it happened.

Upstairs, her mother had probably already read her father the riot act, and she was pretty sure that the only reason she hadn't heard it all go down was the soundproofing in the recording suite. Or maybe Mom hadn't talked to Dad at all. Maybe she'd gotten halfway down the hall, decided to it wasn't a good time to discuss it and gone back to her office to simmer quietly, like a pot of Aunt Gracie's Brunswick stew. She glanced up at the ceiling as if she could see through it, wondering what was going on in the executive suites right now. Knowing she'd find out soon enough how it all had gone down, she returned her attention to the screen.

Behind her, Maxton called her name yet again.

She released a long, drawn-out sigh. It was obvious he wasn't going to go away and leave her in peace to figure out what to do next, so she finally turned her chair around and faced him. "What is there to talk about, Maxton?"

"We need to talk about whatever is going on between us." He gestured with his hands to himself, then to her.

"What we have going on isn't the problem." *Is he really going to make it about us?*

"It's creating a tension between us that is now encroaching on our work, our livelihood. That makes it a problem."

She stared at him, noting the hard set of his jaw and the stiff way he sat, perched on the edge of the sofa. "I don't want to talk about this."

"What is it you're avoiding here, Teagan?" He held her gaze. "I'm trying to get some clarity."

"On what?"

"On why you came in here acting the way you did." He rested his elbows on his thighs, tenting his fingers. "You were so obviously ignoring me that even Swagg picked up on it. You heard what he said to us when he told us to wrap up for the day?"

She rolled her eyes. "Of course. How could I not have heard it, when he was hovering over my workstation?"

He tilted his head slightly to the right. "If you say you heard that, then you should understand that it's a problem, and we should be able to act like adults and talk about it."

"That's pretty big talk, considering the fact that your big mouth just caused a whole lot of trouble for my family."

His expression changed, a crooked half smile flexing his lips. "Oh, I'm the big mouth? You came to me and told me your darkest family secret, but I'm the one with the big mouth?"

She cringed, feeling the sting of his words and of her own regret. "I thought I could trust you. Thought I could unburden myself to you. Apparently, I was wrong."

"See? That's just it." He shook his head. "When I came to you, asking your name, it was because I wanted to know you better. I felt there was a connection between us." He paused, his gaze linking with hers. "You were the one who suggested a fling. No strings, no commitments."

"I know what I said, Maxton." A twinge of tension went up her back, coming to rest between her shoulder blades. She shifted in her chair, attempting to alleviate it, but to no avail.

"Do you? Because when you showed up at my place last night, it sure as hell seemed like you'd forgotten."

She closed her eyes. *I really stepped in it, didn't I? I never should have gone over there.*

"You asked me what I was going to say before I left for my appointment, but the truth is, I'm glad I didn't finish. You're not ready for what I was going to say, and that's crystal clear to me now." He stood, wrapping his fingers around the handle of his instrument case. "I can't do this with you, Teagan."

She felt her heart squeeze in her chest, and she didn't like feeling at all. "Can't do what?"

He gestured around with his free hand. "I don't know—whatever it is we've been doing for the past month."

She felt the squeeze again. "You mean, going on dates? Having deep talks? Making love until we're both exhausted?"

"Yes, that. This fling, or sneaky link, that we've been doing." He sighed. "Call it whatever you want. Either way, I'm out."

She stood, effectively blocking his only exit. "Why? Why don't you want to keep seeing me? Is it because of what happened this morning?"

He shook his head. "No, Teagan, it's all of it. I'm sorry for the awkwardness I caused today, but you gotta realize that even that situation began with you."

She frowned, folding her arms over her chest. "That's not fair."

"I think it's very fair. You dumped the drama in my lap. Otherwise, I wouldn't have known about it. I shouldn't have blurted it out the way I did. That's on me." He shook his head. "But it doesn't matter. This just isn't going to work, and we both know it."

She chewed her lower lip. "I don't see why we can't just renegotiate the terms of our arrangement."

"Because I don't want to, Teagan. I've had enough of this." He drummed his fingers on his instrument case. "I made a mistake in agreeing to the first set of terms, and now it has blown up in both of our faces. It's not the worst mistake I ever made, not by a long shot. But I don't want to make it worse by prolonging it."

"Don't I get a say?" She was pouting and she knew it, but she couldn't control it.

"I've already given you plenty of 'say.' You said you don't want strings or attachments. Those were your words. Well, here's a news flash—if there are no strings, then there are no explanations, either." He fixed her with a penetrating stare. "So when I tell you I'm done, that I don't want this anymore, I shouldn't have to face an inquisition. You should just step aside and let me go."

She swallowed, cursing inwardly at the traitorous tears she felt rising in her throat. "But Maxton…"

He held up his hand. "No. I'm out." He broke eye contact with her and looked past her as if she weren't even in the room anymore. "Now, please step aside."

She angrily wiped away the single tear that fell.

She wanted to change his mind, but that didn't seem likely. So rather than make a fool of herself, she stiffened her spine and gave him a curt nod. "Fine. If that's what you want, then it's over."

"Good. Thank you."

She took a giant step to her right, coming to a stop as her hip bumped up against the counter supporting the workstation.

With the path cleared, Maxton and his bass disappeared through the recording suite's outer door. After he turned the corner, she walked to the door and peered up the corridor. He probably knew she was watching, but he didn't stop, didn't look back, didn't acknowledge her in any way. She caught a fleeting glimpse of his back as he turned the other corner near reception and left the building.

She flopped back into her chair and let the angry tears fall. Part of her felt insulted by the dismissive tone he'd used, and yet another part of her was angry with herself. She knew this was a bad idea from the very beginning; it was why she'd never involved herself with any of the people who came to her suite to work. She'd never dated anyone she worked with, not an artist or producer or manager or session musician. Now that she'd broken that streak, the very first one she'd gotten entangled with turned out to be a dud. *The one time I let my attraction to someone overrule my good sense, this happens. Go, figure.*

It had proven to be a painful mistake, one she didn't plan on making ever again.

She thought about the conversations they'd had, the meals they'd shared, the nights she'd spent lying in his arms. She remembered the way his body felt next to hers, the thrill of having him inside. Was this what it meant to have a fling? To lose yourself in something magical, to the point that you forgot it was only meant to be temporary fun?

Was it supposed to turn out like this, or am I just bad at it? It must be the latter because who would sign up for this? Who would willingly subject themselves to the regret and sadness she felt right now?

Saturday night, Maxton sat at the bar at the Rogue, his hand gripping the handle of a frosty, half-filled mug. Turning it up, he downed the rest of the contents and slammed it down on the counter. "Can I get another?" Nick wasn't working today, but the guy behind the counter seemed cool, nonetheless.

"Number three, coming up." The bartender grabbed his mug, filled it at the tap and slid it back his way.

"Thanks." He grabbed the handle, blowing out a breath. Just a few days ago, everything had been great. He'd had a challenging, well-paid gig with a rising star in hip-hop and a sexy liaison with the world's hottest sound engineer. Now he'd lost one of those things, and as it turned out, it wasn't nearly as expendable as he'd first thought.

The weeks he'd spent with Teagan had been some of the best in his life. Since the loss of his sister, he'd closed himself off from the world, developed a tunnel-vision-like approach to his work, and tried to run from his sorrow. Teagan had made him laugh, made him think. Most of all, she'd made him live again by giving him a reason to get out of his apartment and see what life outside had to offer.

He prepared to hoist the golden liquid to his mouth again but was interrupted by the sound of someone calling his name. Turning his head, he saw a confused-looking Sharrod coming his way.

"Maxton, what the hell's going on with you?"

Maxton shrugged. "Just chilling, man."

"The hell you are." He pointed to the mug. "How many of those have you had?"

"This is my third. But trust me, it won't be my last." He raised the mug in mock salute, then took a deep swig. "Ah, refreshment."

Sharrod didn't appear amused. His face twisted into a sort of disapproving grimace. "I've been calling and texting you all day." He sat down on the stool next to him. "I thought it was weird that you didn't respond, so I went by your place. When you weren't there, my next thought was to check here." He shook his head. "What's going on with you?"

"Nothing. Why were you so pressed to reach me, anyway?"

"Brady and Mike invited us out for the night. You know, drink, eat, maybe hit a club or two." He sucked his teeth. "I see you already got the drinking part started."

He laughed with all the bitterness he felt. "Yeah, I suppose. But I don't wanna go to any club. This here is a party for one." He drained the mug again. "Hey, bartender!"

The bartender returned but paused when Sharrod made eye contact and gave him a solemn head shake. "Sorry, compadre. Maybe dry out a little, okay?"

"Whatever," Maxton groused, shoving his empty mug away. "Thanks a lot for spoiling my fun, Dad."

Sharrod frowned, watching him intently. "You weren't having any fun here, and we both know it."

Maxton shifted his gaze away from his friend's penetrating stare, scratched his nose. "Let me get a ginger ale."

"That, I can do." The bartender whisked the old mug away and soon replaced it with a fresh mug full of the subtly tart soft drink.

"You gonna tell me what happened between you and Ms. Teagan?" Sharrod adjusted his position on the seat.

"I thought you were going to hang out with Mike and Brady tonight?"

"I did, too." He folded his arms over the image of Snoop Dogg on his T-shirt. "But since my homeboy is in trouble, it's been a change of plans. So, speak."

He shook his head, thinking back on their conversation. "I never should have gotten involved with her, man."

"I know that." Sharrod threw up his hands. "I literally told you that from the beginning."

He rolled his eyes. "I bet you're enjoying being right, huh?"

"No, I'm not, for two reasons."

Maxton braced for some smart-ass response, likely accompanied by one of Sharrod's worry anecdotes.

"It's actually kind of weird, being right at this magnitude. Things played out almost exactly as I said they would. That makes it a little too strange to be satisfying."

He drew a deep breath, surprised by the direction this was taking. "What's the other reason?"

Sharrod scratched his chin. "Honestly? It pains me to see you hurting, which you obviously are right now. That takes all the joy out of it. I'm not even gonna say I told you so."

Maxton's brow inched up. "You just did."

"Fair enough, but I won't say it again." Sharrod chuckled. "Anyway, just tell me what happened."

He recounted yesterday's disastrous conversation with Teagan. "Bottom line is, I just can't do this with her. She's asking me for something I just can't give."

"Which is…?" Sharrod eyed him questioningly.

"She wants to keep things casual." He shrugged. "Turns out I can't do that, at least not with her."

Sharrod's brow knit together. "What? Why would you…?" His eyes grew wide. "Bro, you didn't."

In response, Maxton leaned forward, resting his forehead onto the cool marble surface of the bar. "I'm afraid I did."

"Oh, snap." Sharrod's voice was filled with surprise. "I can't believe you fucked around and fell in love."

Maxton felt the groan rising in his throat before it left his mouth. "You and me both. It's the stupidest mess I've ever gotten myself into," he murmured. Before yesterday's ill-fated tête-è-tête, he'd thought the worse part of it was that he'd never gotten to tell Teagan that he loved her. Now he knew better.

Sharrod pursed his lips and blew out a breath. "Damn, that's rough. I do have some good news, though. Maybe it will cheer you up."

"Nothing can cheer me up," Maxton griped, "unless you're willing to let the bartender bring me another beer."

"Come on, Maxton. Hear me out." Sharrod pulled his phone out of his jeans pocket. "When Brady called me, he told me all about it. He's got a connection to a producer out of Houston, through a friend of a friend. Anyway, Brady's producer buddy got him a spot on a nationwide tour. It's an old-school-versus-new-school, festival-type show. This is gonna be epic. I'm talking big names. LL. The Roots crew. That young guy out of Chicago with the blond dreads… Damn, I can't remember his name, but you know who I'm talking about. They even got the Houston hottie herself in the lineup."

Without lifting his head, Maxton sighed. "Sharrod, did you know that when you get excited, you talk fast, and I don't know what the hell you be saying? I got like the first ten words and the rest was gibberish."

Sharrod jabbed him in the shoulder with his finger. "You'd get more of it if you were looking at me while I was talking."

"Sharrod just give me the short version, dude." He dragged himself back up and faced his friend. "You're killing me."

"Short version is this—we have a chance to go on one of the biggest hip-hop tours the country has seen in years. All we gotta do is give our decision by the end of next week so Brady can let the producer know and make the arrangements."

He thought about it. Based on his friend's excitement level and the big names he thought he'd heard him say, it could be a very lucrative gig. "I don't know, man. I'm just not in the right headspace to say yes to this. At least not right now."

Sharrod nodded. "I get it. You gotta work some stuff out." He flagged down the bartender and ordered himself a lemonade. "But I'm definitely gonna take it. I hope you'll be able to come with me."

With a nod, he took a sip from his slightly watered-down soda. Usually, he was quick to say yes to gigs like this. A tour like this was manna from heaven for a working bassist, providing not only income but an opportunity to enjoy some free travel while building relationships that could lead to the next gig.

I just...can't right now. He needed time, time to nurse his bruised heart the same as he'd nursed his black eye, the one he'd gladly taken in Teagan's defense.

"You look a mess, Maxton." Sharrod put his hand on his shoulder. "Look, I'm willing to sit here with you as long as you want. But honestly, I don't think it's the best way to help your situation right now."

"What would you suggest, Sharrod?"

"Let's just go meet up with Brady and Mike. Brady can give you more info about the tour, you can keep drinking without looking sad and pitiful, and we can have some fun." He held up his hands. "I mean, it ain't gonna mend your heart, but the boys and I can certainly dampen the pain for one night."

Maxton locked his hands around his mug, taking a moment to think about it. Sharrod was right, going out with the guys wasn't going to fix it. But neither was sitting here, running up a tab alone. Draining his ginger ale, he pulled out his wallet and tossed down a couple of folded bills to cover his drinks and a tip. "You know what? You're right. Let's go."

Sharrod stood. "Bet."

Sliding off the stool, Maxton did his best to push all thoughts of Teagan Woodson and her beautiful smile out of his mind as he and Sharrod left.

Fourteen

Teagan awakened while it was still dark Monday morning. Glancing around the room, she cursed silently. Too many nights in a row of sleeping like trash were starting to take effect. So she lay there, staring at the ceiling, counting imaginary bunnies jumping over a fence, hoping she'd fall asleep again. By the two hundredth bunny, it became clear that wasn't going to happen. With a deep sigh, she rolled onto her right side and grabbed her phone from the nightstand to check the time.

Five twenty-eight. Great. She usually got up around seven thirty to get dressed and be at the studio by the time it opened at nine. *Looks like I've got some time to kill.*

Free, uncommitted time was the last thing she

wanted right now. Because every moment that she didn't keep busy, her mind filled the space with thoughts of Maxton. She sat up in bed, resting her back against the headboard and yanking the covers up around her neck. Bending her knees, she pulled them close to her body in a sort of upright fetal position. The inky darkness surrounding her felt heavy, oppressive. So she switched on the small lamp on her nightstand and picked up a book she'd been trying to finish.

Her attempt at reading was short-lived, and she soon marked her page and returned the book to its spot on the nightstand. *I doubt Maxton is losing any sleep over me.*

It wasn't a relationship; they weren't soulmates or anything. Or at least, that's what she kept reminding herself every time an image of him popped into her mind. It was just a little harmless fun. But now, as she faced a feeling of loss that she'd never expected, it seemed like much more than that.

It seemed getting tangled up with Maxton had been akin to bringing a kudzu vine into a Georgia forest. It seemed like a swell idea at the time, but the next thing you knew, the vine took over every tree for miles. He was the vine; her heart, the unsuspecting forest.

She finally drifted back to sleep, still sitting up. When she startled awake again, it was almost seven, so she got out of bed and took a hot shower. She was standing in her closet in a bra and panties, rifling through her clothes when she heard her cell phone ringing. Searching through the blankets, she found it on the bed and answered it. "Hello?"

"Teagan." Her mother's voice sounded relieved. "Good, you're up."

"What's up, Mom? Is something wrong?"

"Yes and no. How soon can you get to the building?"

She frowned, confused by her mother's somewhat cryptic words. "Maybe twenty or thirty minutes. Why?"

"Listen carefully. Come to the building as soon as you can. I want you to park, come in through the back door in the courtyard and come directly upstairs to your father's office."

She blinked several times, still processing all of this. "Yes, I can do that. But are you going to tell me what's going on?"

"We'll explain when you get here. Just make sure you do exactly what I say, and don't stop and talk to anyone on the way, okay?"

"I won't. I'll be there as soon as I can."

"Good. Love you."

"Love you, too."

Addison disconnected the call, and Teagan returned to her search for an outfit. Settling on pink blouse and cream-colored slacks made of lightweight material, she got dressed. Stepping into a pair of pink pumps and sliding on a pair of dangly silver earrings fashioned to look like long feathers, she got her purse and keys and left home to drive to the 404 building.

Luckily, the fates granted her a somewhat easy commute through the demolition derby known as Atlanta rush hour traffic, and she made it from her neighborhood in Druid Hills to the building in the northwestern corner of Collier Heights in around twenty-eight minutes.

As she drove down Sound Avenue, the private side street where the company headquarters sat, she saw something odd. Slowing her car near the front of the building, her eyes widened.

What the hell?

There, in the center of the sidewalk, a man reclined in a collapsible camp chair. It was a fancier model of camp chair, with an attached sunshade that enveloped the man's upper body in shadow. He wore dark shorts, a white tee and white sneakers. His face, obscured by a baseball cap and sunglasses, bore a rather silly grin considering the early hour. His legs were extended in front of him, revealing his above-average height, and what looked like a small cooler was set up next to his chair.

Teagan stared as she passed. The man lifted his hand, offering a friendly wave as she drove by.

Shaking her head, she pulled around to the side lot, turned in and parked as close as she could to the courtyard. After locking up the car, she entered the rear door using her keycard, then took the elevator upstairs to the fourth floor.

Entering her father's office, she found her parents inside. Her mother sat on the right side of the room, near the bookcases, while her father stood at the window behind his desk, peering out.

Addison stood when her daughter entered. "Hey, Teagan. Thanks for coming in early."

"You're welcome. Does anybody want to tell me what's going on? Because there's a man on the sidewalk in front, and he looks pretty dang comfortable."

"We know," her father called over his shoulder. "It's him."

"Who?" Teagan looked from her father to her mother and back again before realization hit her like a wet towel across the backside "Oh, snap. It's—"

"Yes. It's Keegan Woodbine, the crazy person who claims to be my son." Caleb shook his head. "The nerve of him, showing up here at my place of business."

Addison snorted. "It's your fault he's here."

"Addy, I told you already. I don't have any other children. It simply isn't possible."

Addison slapped her hand down on the small table she'd been sitting at. "Then, damn it, Caleb, go tell him that. Go down there and talk to him."

Caleb bristled. "I don't want to talk to him."

"And I don't want to call the police on him, either, because we all know how that could end." Addison sat down in the chair, her shoulders drooping.

"He's smart, I see." Teagan walked closer to her

mother. "He set himself up on the sidewalk because it's just beyond our property line."

"Right." Addison shook her head sadly. "Caleb, this is the last time I'm going to say this. Carry your stubborn ass down there and talk to that boy. I'm not gonna have him sitting here when Lil Swagg and his musicians start arriving."

"Addy…"

"If you 'Addy' me one more time…" Her voice was hard, cold. "Get out. Go deal with him, or he'll be the least of your worries."

Caleb sighed. Straightening his sports coat, he left the room.

Teagan grabbed her mother's hand, gave it a squeeze. "Mom, are you okay?"

"No." She ran her free hand over her face. "I waited to talk to your father about this until we were at home because I didn't want to cause a scene. He spent all weekend telling me it's not true, that it's impossible. We came in early this morning to inventory the storage room, and that boy was already sitting there."

Teagan asked, "Why did you call me?"

"Because you're the only child that knows about this mess so far, and I don't want to pull your sister and brothers into it any sooner than I have to." She blinked rapidly, tears welling in her eyes. "This whole thing is so upsetting."

Teagan bent and hugged her mother tight around her drooping shoulders. "It's going to be okay,

Mom, Somehow." Easing away from her mother, she walked to the window. She could see Caleb talking to Keegan, who'd stood and folded his chair. Both men appeared calm, at least from her vantage point, but there was no telling what they were saying to each other.

"What's going on out there?" Addison asked.

"They're talking. Calmly, from the looks of it." They went back and forth for a few minutes, then Caleb watched while Keegan packed up his chair and his cooler and crossed the street. Caleb started back toward the building, and Teagan watched Keegan climb into a Jeep parked at the dry cleaners across the road and drive off.

Caleb returned to the office, swinging the door closed behind him. "There. The problem is solved."

Addison looked at her husband with narrowed eyes. "Just like that, eh. And how do you figure it's solved, Caleb?"

"He showed me a birth certificate with my name on it as his father." He shrugged. "That's far too easy to fabricate, so I dismissed it."

"And how did he react to that?" Addison pressed.

"He seemed offended, but I certainly didn't care. I demanded a DNA test. I told him that if he could prove he was my son, we'd sit down and talk about his inheritance." He eased over to his desk and seated himself in the big executive chair, looking rather self-satisfied. "That was enough to get him to leave."

Addison rose slowly from her seat. "You told me it's not possible for him to be your son."

"It's not." Caleb picked up a pen from the cup on his desk and tapped it his forehead. "That's why I agreed to do the test. Once we have concrete proof, you'll be reassured that I'm telling the truth, and he won't have a leg to stand on to make any further claims."

Addison stared at her husband but didn't utter a single word.

Teagan swallowed, sensing her mother's rising anger. She sidled closer to her, locking an arm around her waist. "Mom, let's go get a cup of coffee."

"Sure, honey." Her voice dripped with false pleasantry. "But first, let me tell your father something." She took two steps closer to his desk, resting her palms on the other side. "There is no way I can explain to you how hurt and embarrassed I am. You knew, for weeks, about this accusation, and you hid it from me. Now you think everything is fine." Her words dripped with icy intent. "You may think your problem with that boy is over. Your problems with me, however, are just beginning." She stood, turned and sailed out.

Unsure of what else to do, Teagan followed her mother and closed the door behind her.

Keeping his eyes focused on the cars flowing around him, Maxton navigated the gauntlet to reach the designated pickup area of Hartsfield-Jackson Atlanta International Airport on Monday evening. He couldn't think of anyone else he'd go through the trouble for, other than his parents. So when his dad had called, he'd sucked it up and prepared to make the drive.

Scanning the sidewalk in front of the terminal doors, he saw a woman in profile. Her little black dress, bouncy curls and long legs reminded him of Teagan, and he sighed aloud. Working with her today had been difficult, to say the least, but he'd put on his blinders and focused on the work at hand. As a result, track nine of Swagg's album had now been completed, and only two tracks remained before they could officially put this project in the books. Shaking off those thoughts of her smile, and of the tears he'd seen standing in her eyes when he broke things off, he went back to searching for his father.

After a few more laps around the pickup zone, he finally spotted his dad. Dr. Stephen McCoy, clad in his starched khaki shorts and matching short-sleeved shirt, stood out among the more comfortably dressed travelers. Maxton slipped into the nearest empty spot and got out, opening the hatch.

"Hey, Dad," he said, reaching for a hug.

Stephen smiled and embraced his son. "Evening, son. Good to see you."

Maxton took his father's two duffle bags and tucked them carefully into the back. Closing the hatch, he got into the driver's seat, buckled up and pulled away from the curb.

They drove through the city, headed back toward Maxton's place. "So, how was the flight?"

"Long." Stephen chuckled. "International flights are always like that, though. Luckily, I booked a first-class seat that folds into a bed, so it wasn't too bad."

Maxton nodded. "Any idea what you want to eat?"

"Something other than Italian," he quipped. "I've had my fill of pasta over these last couple of weeks."

"I got you." He chuckled, glad he'd made other arrangements for his father's brief visit.

Later, at his apartment, Maxton whipped up a simple, classic-Southern feast for his father. When he presented him with the plate of fried chicken wings, cinnamon waffles and green beans seasoned with onions, his father whistled. "Wow, son. When did you learn to cook like this?"

He shrugged, sitting next to his father on the sofa, holding his own plate. "Being on the road as much as I am, takeout gets old quick. So I took some time between tours to learn how to cook for myself."

"Wise decision." Stephen munched on a wing, the crisp skin crackling as he chewed.

"I take a few shortcuts here and there. Like using frozen waffles." He winked.

His father laughed. "Hey, I'll allow it."

"So, tell me," Maxton said, sipping from his glass of iced water, "what kinds of cool stuff did you come across on your trip? Mom told me you were itching to get to the Valley of Temples."

"I was, and I've made some very interesting finds over there." Stephen clasped his hands together. "I'm so glad I finally got the chance to go."

Maxton settled back against the cushions. He loved hearing about his parent's travels, and now he could use any distraction he could get from thinking about Teagan. "Alright, let me hear it."

"I spent most of my time on the western end of the valley. There's a garden down there, called the Garden of the Kolymbethra. It's huge—five hectares. That's over ten acres. Anyway, this place is so lush. It has so many varieties of trees—white poplar, willow, myrtle, broom. Then, there's an orchard full of citrus trees. They have almonds and olives and so much good stuff growing there." He smiled. "I just wish your mother could have gone to see it. She'd love it. I'm gonna go back, take her with me, when I get around to it."

"I think that's a great idea. She'd probably love that."

"I also spent a good amount of time exploring the ruins of the Temple of Castor and Pollux. That place is huge. It's a two-mile walk just to cover the span of the inside. I was able to collect a few soil samples as well as some fragments we think might be ancient pottery. We tagged everything, turned it over to the proper authorities for analysis."

"How long will it take to find out what it was?"

He shrugged. "Few weeks to months. I'm a patient man. I can wait." He scraped up the last of his green beans. "Enough of my adventures. What's going on with you? Are you enjoying your time in Atlanta?"

He thought about how he'd answer. "It's been mostly good. I've really been enjoying this gig. Sharrod and I are working with a rapper out of the Bronx who brought in a full band for his next album. It's really been an experience."

Stephen nodded slowly. "Okay. Now, tell me what's not going so well."

"I…got involved in something I shouldn't have."

His gray brow arched. "Is it legal, son?"

"Yeah." He chuckled, in spite of his somewhat somber mood. "I realize now how that must have sounded. What I meant was, I got into a sort of romantic entanglement, and I'd have probably been better off just walking away in the beginning."

"Oh, now I definitely want to hear about this." Stephen shifted in his seat, resting his back against the armrest and faced his son. "Tell me about this woman."

"Her name is Teagan, and she's the head sound engineer at the studio where I've been working."

"Lord have mercy. Not a workplace fling."

Maxton cringed. "I'm afraid so." He recounted the story of his brief affair with Teagan in as much detail as he felt was appropriate to tell his father. Starting with that first day, when he'd asked her his name, he described their time together up until last Friday when he'd broken things off. "I could tell I wanted more than she was willing to give, and I didn't want to stick around and get my heart stepped on."

Stephen scratched his chin. "So what you're saying is you weren't supposed to be together in the first place, but you couldn't resist her. And now, even though you're apart, you realized you love her. Is that right?"

"I never said I loved her, Dad."

"Maxton, you didn't have to. If you didn't love her, you wouldn't be struggling with the situation the way you are." Stephen shook his head. "Did I ever tell you how your mother and I met?"

"She told me you met at UC Santa Cruz."

"We did." He nodded. "But did she tell you that we started out competing against each other for a single scholarship to the humanities department?" He looked off into the distance. "I first saw her on the quad, the summer before sophomore year. I asked her out and took her on two dates before I found out."

"And how did that go down?"

"We had to give a presentation to the award committee, as a last step in the process of potentially earning the scholarship, which was for upperclassmen in humanities. I'd already given my speech when your mother came running into the auditorium. She was late for the presentation. But she still got up there and nailed it."

Maxton leaned in. "Okay, so did she fuss you out?"

He shook his head. "No. I fussed her out, idiot that

I was. Told her I couldn't see her anymore. I blew my presentation and I blamed her for it. She was a 'distraction,' or at least that's what I told myself. I still can't believe I said that to her."

Now the parallel between these stories was becoming much clearer.

"I spent the next three weeks throwing myself into work, miserable. I lost her and I lost the scholarship. But you know what? Your mom won it. Even though she was late, she made a hell of a presentation. Won the committee over just like that." He snapped his fingers. "When I finally got my head out of my behind, I crawled back to her and asked her to be my girlfriend. Lucky for me, and for you, your mother's forgiving spirit overrode her annoyance with me. By the time school started in the fall, we were an item."

Maxton whistled. "I see you two got off to a rocky start."

"We did. But I'm glad I had sense enough to realize how important she was to me before she got away."

He thought about that for a moment, thought about how he would feel if Teagan found someone else. How would he be able to accept that, knowing he hadn't even told her how he felt? "I don't want that. Dad. I don't want Teagan to be the one that got away."

"Then, I think you know what you have to do." He stood, gathering their plates. "Listen, son. I'm not going to tell you what to do. You're a grown man.

But I will say this. If you really love her, you'd better tell her that." He stood in the arched doorway leading to the kitchen, his gaze intent. "Sometimes, you have to be willing to go to a woman with your hat in your hand and tell her you were wrong. And there's no shame in it."

As his father washed the dinner dishes, Maxton let his head drop back, his gaze resting on the ceiling. He'd understand if Teagan told him to kick rocks, but he had to at least try. No other woman had ever made him feel the way she did, and he didn't want to walk away, didn't want to wait and see if someone better came along.

He wanted Teagan.

I love her. Now I just have to figure out how to get her back.

Fifteen

Munching on the last bit of a croissant, Teagan stood in the hallway just outside Studio One. It was Tuesday morning, and she'd just arrived to prepare for today's recording session. Only two tracks remained to be finished on Lil Swagg's album, and she hoped they'd finish this week. If they didn't, she'd have to call the next artist who'd booked use of the studio and see if they were willing to move up their slot so Swagg could have more time.

Hopefully, these next few days would be super productive.

Draining the last of the coffee in the paper cup she'd brought from the Bodacious Bean, she tossed the empty cup and the crumpled pastry wrapper into the trash, dusted off her hands and entered the studio.

She was seated at the workstation a few minutes later when Swagg and Rick walked in. She waved to them as they headed for their usual perch on the sofa while continuing to let the workstation run through its daily start-up protocols.

The musicians began trickling in with Mike arriving around nine thirty and Brady around a quarter till. Five minutes before ten, Sharrod entered, drumsticks in hand.

Teagan surreptitiously watched the door without taking her eyes off the screen, knowing Maxton wouldn't be too far behind.

A few long seconds passed.

Finally, she saw someone entering, their face obscured behind a huge bouquet of orchids.

Her heart turned a flip when she saw the vase lower to reveal Maxton's handsome face and the huge grin he wore. "Good morning."

"Morning," she stammered, captivated by the beauty of the blooms. "What's…all this?" She gestured to the flowers.

"That would be thirty Ocean Breeze orchids," he said, handing the clear crystal vase to her. "Your brother was kind enough to tell me orchids are your favorite flower."

She frowned, confused. "Which brother? Gage?"

He shook his head. "No. Miles."

She gasped. "Wow. I've never known my twin to like any guy well enough to help him out with that sort of thing."

Miles peeked his head around the door frame at that precise moment. "You're right. I deeply dislike most men who try to date you." He patted Maxton on the shoulder. "But this guy makes a hell of a case for himself. Give him a chance, sis." With a wink, he strolled off toward the elevators.

Maxton jerked his thumb in the direction Miles had appeared from. "How's that for an endorsement?"

She giggled. "It's pretty damn good." She looked him over, taking in the black jeans, distressed black tee shirt and the black-and-white bandana tied around his forehead, keeping his curls out of his face.

He squatted, hanging on to the armrest of her chair as he came to her eye level. "I wanted to apologize for the way I acted Friday."

She shook her head, feeling the tears form in her eyes. "No, you were right. I contradicted myself and put way too much on you, considering the parameters I set."

He grabbed her hand. "But that's just it. I don't want parameters with you, Teagan. I want it all. All the secrets, all the excitement, even all the sorrow. You're too special for a fling or an affair."

"And what makes you say that?"

"I love you, Teagan." He squeezed her hand inside his own. "I don't even know when it happened. Maybe it was the first time I saw you, working so hard and looking all serious. Or maybe it was the smile on your face when I took you to swim with the rays. Or maybe, it happened that day in Piedmont Park, when we kissed in the rain."

She was full-on crying by now. "Damn it, Maxton. I'm gonna look like a raccoon if you keep this up."

"Sorry 'bout that, baby. Rest in peace to your mascara." He brushed away a few tears from her cheek. "Anyway, it doesn't matter when or how it happened. All I know is that I love you, and I want a full relationship with you. Give me all the stings, all the commitments. I'm ready."

"You have no idea how relieved I am to hear this," she said, sniffling. "Because I love you, too, Maxton." He drew her into his arms and held her tight while everyone in the studio cheered.

"That's what I'm talking about! Get ya lady, homeboy!" Swagg's exuberant declaration rose above every other sound in the space, and Teagan laughed as she pulled back from the hug.

A smiling Maxton reached into the hip pocket of his jeans and pulled out a small box.

She drew back. "You didn't."

He laughed. "No, I didn't. I'm not about to jump straight to the proposal, I mean, unless…"

She punched him in the shoulder.

"Ouch." He rubbed the shoulder, feigning injury. "It's not a ring. It's this." He opened the small blue box and held it up so she could see the contents.

She sucked in a breath. "Oh, my."

Inside the velvet interior was a beautiful charm

bracelet with alternating silver and gold beads. Three charms dangled from it: a sea turtle, a great white shark and a stingray. She lifted it out of the box, admiring its beauty and detail work up close. "This is gorgeous. Thank you so much."

"You're welcome. You do understand that if you put that on, you're officially my girlfriend."

She slipped the bracelet over her hand and onto her wrist without a moment's hesitation. "Good. Because that's just what I want."

He pulled her close again, but this time, he kissed her on the lips. The hoots and hollers of the men present filled her ears, but she didn't care. She couldn't remember the last time she'd felt so happy, so at peace.

Eventually, they parted, and Maxton grabbed his bass from the hallway and took it into the booth, and she turned her chair back around to face the workstation and clicked on the intercom. "You guys ready to finish this album and make it a hit?"

Swagg was on his feet, and he strolled up to the partition with a broad grin. "Listen. With all these good feelings and good vibes floating around the room right now—" he paused, giving Teagan's shoulder a gentle pat "—I think we should be able to just knock out these last two tracks right now, today. You feel me?"

The band seemed to agree, based on their boisterous reactions.

Laughing, Teagan said, "Okay, boys. Let's get it."

Touching her screen, she started playback on track ten's melody file.

Swagg's proclamation turned out to be right, because the day quickly became a real, honest-to-goodness jam session. Bobbing her head along to the music, Teagan could feel the rhythmic energy flowing through the space. It seemed as if the good vibes Swagg had described, vibes she was at least partially responsible for creating, were fueling the musicians to play at the top of their skills. They ran through a few versions of each track and found the sweet spot where Swagg, his manager and the musicians were happy. That done, everyone left the booth and congregated in the outer suite to watch Swagg as he laid down his verses over the album's last two tracks.

"Looks like Swagg is feeling the flow today, too," Rick quipped as his artist effortlessly laid down bar after bar. He did so well, he was able to record his verses on both finished musical tracks in only a single continuous take.

By 4:00 p.m., Teagan had completed the final file cleanup and combined all the finished audio files into a folder. She turned to Swagg. "As soon as you tell me where to send these, you can consider your album finished."

Rick slid her a card. "Send everything to Chanel the Titan, and cc it to Big Apple Records. Here are the website addresses to the encrypted upload portals."

"You got it." Teagan set to work on the uploads. "So, Swagg, does the album have a title yet?"

He shook his head. "Nothing official, but I can feel some ideas forming in my brain. Gotta give them some time to marinate."

"I can't wait to hear what you come up with." She reached out and shook his hand. "Thank you so much for the opportunity to work with you on this project. I'm really proud of how it turned out."

"So am I." Swagg turned to Rick. "Let's go celebrate, man."

Rick clapped his hands together. "I'm definitely down for that." He looked to the band members. "You guys coming?"

Everyone filed out of the room, with Sharrod hanging back to fist-bump Maxton. "Catch up with us later." With a wink, Sharrod disappeared out the door.

Standing in the doorway of the booth, Maxton smiled at Teagan. "What a day, right?"

"Right. It's been a wild ride." She raised her wrist, admiring the way her bracelet caught the light. "Where on earth did you find these sea-life charms?"

"I made it to the jewelry store last night before it closed." He approached her chair. "I couldn't believe they had those charms for my girl."

She could feel the grin spreading across her face. "That's me. I'm your girl."

He gently tugged her out of her chair and into his strong arms. "All mine."

She didn't know what it was about his posessive tone that seemed to touch her like a caress, but as their lips met, she realized she didn't really care.

Ten Weeks Later
Houston, TX

Maxton kept his eyes straight ahead, effectively staring at LL Cool J's legendary back as he plucked out the bassline to the rapper's 1995 hit, "Loungin." Because this was the last show on the Hip-Hop Classic vs Current Tour, the members of the nineties girl group Total had joined LL on the stage, to reprise their harmonies on the song's catchy hook.

Sweat ran down his face, a common predicament when he played under stage lights for hours at stretch, but he paid it no mind. This was what he loved most, performing with an artist he respected, in front of a crowd of true fans.

As the tune ended and LL walked offstage to the roars of the crowd, Maxton set his bass down and flexed his fingers.

"Hell of a night," Sharrod shouted from his seat behind the drums set.

"Yeah," Maxton called back, nodding. "That's how you close up a tour."

The stage lights went down as the curtain dropped, and Maxton carefully placed his bass inside the case and snapped it shut. Carrying it with him, he walked off the stage, headed for the greenroom.

Passing some of the artists on his way down the narrow corridor, he waved to them. Finally arriving, he opened the greenroom door.

Teagan sat on the black leather sofa, her open laptop on her thighs. Her hair was up in a messy bun on top of her head, revealing the graceful line of her jawline and neck. Dressed in dark-wash skinny jeans and a sparkly silver tank top with black ballet flats, she looked both stylish and comfortable. "Hey, you."

"Hey, baby." He walked over, propping his bass on a stand in the corner and flopping down on the couch next to her. Giving her a quick kiss, he asked, "What are you up to?"

"Just got off a video chat with Nia. She's ready for me to come home. She says Luna misses me."

"She's guilt-tripping you with your cat? I'm guessing she wants you back at work?"

She laughed. "Yes. Trevor's been running both studios, and apparently, the engineer the temp agency sent over to help him isn't up to par."

"Are you ready to go back?"

She shrugged. "I mean, I miss Luna. And I don't like other sound engineers touching Fancy. She's mine. Plus, I've never taken this much time off work before, so I can understand why they'd be floundering without me."

"I guess they really need you around, huh?" He kissed her again. "I'm still glad you decided to come on the road with me for a few weeks. Having you here has made the last part of the tour even more amazing."

She smiled, and he melted inside. "I'm glad I came, too. I needed a little adventure in my life. Nia was right. I work too hard."

"Well, it's officially the end of the tour, so we can hop an early flight back to Atlanta tomorrow." He stopped, hearing the muffled sound of the crowd as it seemed to rise again. "I guess folks are still out there."

Sharrod walked in, still clutching his sticks. "We're on, bro. Crowd wants an encore."

Maxton stood. "Looks like I'm on again. Why don't you watch from backstage this time?"

"Sure. I'm game." She shut her laptop, tossing it into her large purse. Slinging the purse over her shoulder, she followed them back down the corridor. Taking up a post near the stage crew, she stopped and watched as they returned to their places on stage.

Maxton was seated on his stool, bass in hand, when the curtain rose again. The DJ dropped the intro to LL's classic, "I Need Love," and the man himself returned to the stage to the sounds of loud cheers and thunderous applause.

The DJ spoke into his mic. "Y'all know this jam is about something we all need. Right, Uncle L?" LL raised his mic, nodding his head to the music.

"That's right, so let's give some love to our band tonight. Y'all know me, DJ Bigg Stuff, on the ones and the twos. Let's give it up for my man, Brady, on the guitar."

The crowd cheered as the DJ went on to name each musician individually, then gave them a few seconds to show off before moving on to the next. Maxton watched as Sharrod played his drum solo, and took a deep breath, knowing he was next.

"And last but not least, we got my man Maxton McCoy on the bass. Take it away, Max."

Max stood as the spotlight landed on him, but instead of playing a bass solo, he took the mic Sharrod handed him and spoke into it. "Y'all good out there tonight?" Pausing a moment for the crowd's roar, he raised the mic to his lips again. "Our illustrious DJ is right. We all need love. And when you find it, you better hold on tight." He gestured, and a burly stagehand escorted the bewildered-looking Teagan out on the stage.

Teagan stood in front of him, her eyes the size of a bass drum, and mouthed, "What's going on?"

He took her hand. "Y'all see this fine woman? She got my heart on lockdown. And today, I'm trying to make it all the way official, right here in front of the great city of Houston."

Teagan's hand began to shake inside his. He dropped to one knee, pulling the black box out of his pocket. Popping the lid open, he held up the brilliant cut, teardrop-shaped two-carat diamond ring for her to see. "Teagan Woodson, will you marry me?"

Her lips trembled, the tears streaming down her cheeks illuminated by the spotlight. Taking the mic, she spoke into it. "Yes, Maxton."

The crowd roared, the band cheered, even LL clapped for them as Maxton slipped the ring on her finger. Once that was done, he stood and drew her into his arms for a kiss. They ran offstage, finding a dark, semi-quiet corner away from the noise and the prying eyes. There, they embraced again, kissing passionately.

She pulled back, looking up into his eyes, with tears sparkling in her own. "I can't believe you did all this."

"Believe it. A woman like you deserves something really special. I just hope I pulled it off well enough."

She gave his waist a squeeze. "Trust me, you did everything just right." She touched his face. "I love you, Maxton McCoy."

"I love you too, baby."

She leaned up to kiss him again, and time seemed to stand still. Being with her felt natural because her love provided the most perfect melody to complement his bassline.

And he couldn't wait to experience the beautiful music they would make together.

* * * * *

#2887 RIVALRY AT PLAY

Texas Cattleman's Club: Ranchers and Rivals
by Nadine Gonzalez

Attorney Alexandra Lattimore isn't looking for love. She's home to help her family—and to escape problems at work. But sparks with former rival Jackson Strom are too hot to resist. Will her secrets keep them from rewriting their past?

#2888 THEIR MARRIAGE BARGAIN

Dynasties: Tech Tycoons • by Shannon McKenna

If biotech tycoon Caleb Moss isn't married soon, he'll lose control of the family company. Ex Tilda Riley's unexpected return could solve his marriage bind—in name only. But can this convenient arrangement withstand the heat between them?

#2889 A COLORADO CLAIM

Return to Catamount • by Joanne Rock

Returning home to defend her inheritance, Lark Barclay is surprised to see her ex-husband, rancher Gibson Vaughn. And Gibson proves hard to ignore. She's out to claim her land, but will he reclaim her heart?

#2890 CROSSING TWO LITTLE LINES

by Joss Wood

When heiress Jamie Bacall and blue-collar billionaire Rowan Cowper meet in an elevator, a hot, no-strings fling ensues. But when Jamie learns she's pregnant, will their relationship cross the line into something more?

#2891 THE NANNY GAME

The Eddington Heirs • by Zuri Day

Running his family's empire is a full-time job, so when a baby is dropped off at his estate, Desmond Eddington needs nanny Ivy Campbell. Escaping painful pasts, neither is open to love, but it's impossible to ignore their attraction...

#2892 BLAME IT ON VEGAS

Bad Billionaires • by Kira Sinclair

Avid card shark Luca Kilpatrick hasn't returned to the casino since Annalise Mercado's family accused him of cheating. But now he's the only one who can catch a thief—if he can resist the chemistry that's too strong to deny...

Finding his father's assistant at an underground fight club, playboy Mason Kane realizes he isn't the only one leading a double life. So he offers Charlotte Westbrook a whirlwind Riviera fling to help her loosen up, but it could cost her job and her heart...

Read on for a sneak peek at
Secret Lives After Hours
by Cynthia St. Aubin

They stood facing each other, the summer heat still radiating up from the sidewalk, the sultry breath of a coming storm sifting through their hair.

Now.

Now was the moment where she would pull out her phone, bring up the ride app. Bid him good-night. If she did this, the past three hours could be bundled into a box neither of them would ever have to open again. He might smile at her secretively every now and then, wink at her in acknowledgment, but that would be the end of it.

If she left now.

"Come up," Mason said.

It wasn't a question. It wasn't even an invitation.

It was an answer.

HDEXP0622

An answer to her own admission in the elevator. That she liked looking at him. That she could look at him more if she wanted.

That he wanted her to.

"Okay," Charlotte said.

Don't miss what happens next in…
Secret Lives After Hours *by Cynthia St. Aubin,*
the next book in The Kane Heirs series!
Available August 2022 wherever
Harlequin Desire books and ebooks are sold.

Harlequin.com

Get 4 FREE REWARDS!

We'll send you 2 FREE Books plus 2 FREE Mystery Gifts.

FREE Value Over **$20**

Both the **Harlequin® Desire** and **Harlequin Presents®** series feature compelling novels filled with passion, sensuality and intriguing scandals.

YES! Please send me 2 FREE novels from the Harlequin Desire or Harlequin Presents series and my 2 FREE gifts (gifts are worth about $10 retail). After receiving them, if I don't wish to receive any more books, I can return the shipping statement marked "cancel." If I don't cancel, I will receive 6 brand-new Harlequin Presents Larger-Print books every month and be billed just $5.80 each in the U.S. or $5.99 each in Canada, a savings of at least 11% off the cover price or 6 Harlequin Desire books every month and be billed just $4.55 each in the U.S. or $5.24 each in Canada, a savings of at least 13% off the cover price. It's quite a bargain! Shipping and handling is just 50¢ per book in the U.S. and $1.25 per book in Canada.* I understand that accepting the 2 free books and gifts places me under no obligation to buy anything. I can always return a shipment and cancel at any time. The free books and gifts are mine to keep no matter what I decide.

Choose one: ☐ **Harlequin Desire**
(225/326 HDN GNND)

☐ **Harlequin Presents Larger-Print**
(176/376 HDN GNWY)

Name (please print)

Address   Apt. #

City   State/Province   Zip/Postal Code

Email: Please check this box ☐ if you would like to receive newsletters and promotional emails from Harlequin Enterprises ULC and its affiliates. You can unsubscribe anytime.

Mail to the **Harlequin Reader Service:**
IN U.S.A.: P.O. Box 1341, Buffalo, NY 14240-8531
IN CANADA: P.O. Box 603, Fort Erie, Ontario L2A 5X3

Want to try 2 free books from another series? Call 1-800-873-8635 or visit www.ReaderService.com.

*Terms and prices subject to change without notice. Prices do not include sales taxes, which will be charged (if applicable) based on your state or country of residence. Canadian residents will be charged applicable taxes. Offer not valid in Quebec. This offer is limited to one order per household. Books received may not be as shown. Not valid for current subscribers to the Harlequin Presents or Harlequin Desire series. All orders subject to approval. Credit or debit balances in a customer's account(s) may be offset by any other outstanding balance owed by or to the customer. Please allow 4 to 6 weeks for delivery. Offer available while quantities last.

Your Privacy—Your information is being collected by Harlequin Enterprises ULC, operating as Harlequin Reader Service. For a complete summary of the information we collect, how we use this information and to whom it is disclosed, please visit our privacy notice located at corporate.harlequin.com/privacy-notice. From time to time we may also exchange your personal information with reputable third parties. If you wish to opt out of this sharing of your personal information, please visit readerservice.com/consumerschoice or call 1-800-873-8635. **Notice to California Residents**—Under California law, you have specific rights to control and access your data. For more information on these rights and how to exercise them, visit corporate.harlequin.com/california-privacy.

HDHP22